DAMAGE, HEALING, LOVE

CONNOR WHITELEY

No part of this book may be reproduced in any form or by any electronic or mechanical means. Including information storage, and retrieval systems, without written permission from the author except for the use of brief quotations in a book review.

This book is NOT legal, professional, medical, financial or any type of official advice.

Any questions about the book, rights licensing, or to contact the author, please email connorwhiteley@connorwhiteley.net

Copyright © 2024 CONNOR WHITELEY

All rights reserved.

DEDICATION

Thank you to all my readers without you I couldn't do what I love.

CHAPTER 1

23rd January 2024

Canterbury, England

"Why are we going to this Fair thing?"

Zach James just laughed and pulled his best friend, Lora, in the entire world in for a massive hug as they went up a long terribly tarmacked path with thick oak, pine and beech trees lining it. He shivered a little as he watched his breathe condense and formed thick columns of vapour.

He sort of felt like a dragon. He breathed heavily and just smiled as the thick columns shot out his nose. The air was great with hints of grass, damp and freshly cut wood that only helped to make the day even better.

Zach had always really liked the smell of cut wood. It reminded him of being home with his Mum, Dad and two brothers who helped their Dad on their tree farm. Zach had never actually cared too much about the farm but it was sustainably done so he supposed he shouldn't have minded that much.

The sky above was grey but at least it wasn't going to rain and it wasn't wet. Zach really didn't like going out when it was wet and cold, it was so draining and there was nothing better than being in-doors with friends and a boyfriend.

Not that Zach actually had a boyfriend even more because of... an old friend called Jayden. Zach shook the thought away because thinking about Jayden, what they had done to each other and how innocent Jayden was, was never a good idea.

"Why?" Lora asked like a small child.

Zach shook his head and just smiled at his best friend. She always did look great with her long blond hair that ran down to the top of her legs, her green jacket showed off her thin body and she was really fun to be around.

She was brilliant, but she clearly didn't see the benefit of going to the Big Fair.

"Because I want to look at the Societies, which before you ask because I know you're a big kid at heart. They are what the university calls adult social clubs and no I do not know, why they are called Societies," Zach said.

They both smiled and Zach focused back on the tarmacked path. It was rather nice not seeing any other students on it, normally when he went to his lectures the path was packed full of students and it was a free for all.

It was even worse when it was raining or had just

rained. And the wide stretches of grass to the side of the path turned into mud baths and sadly the trees provided little to no cover.

The sound of birds, cars and students in the far distance made Zach realise they were coming up to the university campus. The last time he had been up this path was before Winter Break so he hadn't realised how far and close everything was at different points.

"Why do you want us to do a society together?" Lora asked. "We already spent so much time together, so why don't you admit the real reason you want me to come along?"

Zach forced himself not to stop in his tracks, so he kept on walking. He didn't want to tell Lora how he had been spending so much time with her and still wanted to be with her constantly just so he didn't have to think about Ryan. Ryan had left him, shattered his heart and just wrecked him because of what Jayden had innocently done.

Zach shook his head. He couldn't start thinking about Jayden and what had happened last August. It wasn't healthy. It wasn't good and he would only start getting depressed again.

He couldn't go back to that place, so he lied.

"The real reason is because we have both been living in my flat and talking with my flatmates for the past four months. We need to get out and see people," Zach said.

"Sure, sure," Lora said smiling.

"It's the truth and I know we both have other friends, and once a week we go out to Q-Bar with six people. But I want to actually *do* something more,"

Lora laughed. "Darling, you haven't *done* anyone for two months,"

Zach flinched a little and tried to grin and smile. It didn't really work and he was going to have to tell Lora that he didn't want reminders of Ryan. It was true him and Ryan had been very active in the bedroom and Ryan had left him in November after struggling for months.

He just didn't need to be reminders of it.

"I am sorry you know. I really am and I won't mention it again," Lora said knowing he didn't like reminders of Ryan. "How about we look at a baking society? We both like baking, right?"

Zach laughed as they went towards a little black path that shot away from the one they were currently on. It was a shortcut towards the Sports Hall where the Big Fair was happening.

Zach had no idea if he actually liked Baking or not because he had never tried it. But if it meant meeting new people, making new friends and getting out back into the world then he was certainly up for it.

And that excited him a lot more than he ever wanted to admit.

5

CHAPTER 2
23rd January 2024

Canterbury, England

University student Jayden Baker was so excited as he laid on his back on his soft, warm, cosy single bed in his university flat. He couldn't wait for his friends to knock on his door so they could go to The Big Fair together at the university. An event that Jayden really hoped would allow him to join new social groups, new activities and meet new people.

Maybe even a boyfriend.

Jayden sat up a little on his bed and hissed a little as the icy coldness of the flat's white walls chilled him a lot more than he wanted to admit. He had only gotten back to Kent University last week but he was still getting used to the cold winters. And how the university's apartment buildings failed to keep out much of the cold.

Jayden really liked the flat though. It might have been a bit pricey (which was why his parents were thankfully paying for it), but it was great and it was home. He was so glad the university had allowed him to put up some of his favourite landscape photos that he had taken. He had loved the trips from the hilly landscapes of Wales and the rough coastline of Cornwall and the stunning sunsets he had gotten in the Lake District.

He flat out loved photography and managing to actually capture a moment like the viewer was really there. That was the whole point of taking a photo.

Jayden heard a hiss as his automatic air fresher (a little Christmas gift from his mother) was activated. He still needed to find out how to turn the silly thing off but he liked the calming notes of fig and amber and there were some hints there that he wasn't too sure about. They were probably violet and jasmine but he wasn't sure, but they did smell great.

He could almost taste the great fig pie his grandmother used to make. Jayden had always loved that as a kid with whipped cream, strawberries and the most intense vanilla ice cream he had ever tasted.

A buzzing sound filled the flat.

Jayden leant across the tiny gap that was between his bed and his wooden "desk". That was actually nothing more than a very nice sheet of walnut wood that stretched the entire length of the flat (all five metres of it) with a desk chair. Not a traditional desk but Jayden didn't mind.

Jayden picked up his phone and took out the charger. He grinned as his best friends in the entire world Caroline, Kate and Jackie were coming to his flat now. Jayden was glad he was going to see them because he hadn't seen them since they went up North for the winter break.

Jayden wasn't exactly sure why he wanted to go to the Big Fair. It was a massive event where all the social group or Societies as they preferred to be called, got to advertise themselves again and students could see them.

He had gone to Freshers' fair back in September, but Jayden tensed a little because that really wasn't the best time to look for new, stressful and scary events.

Jayden hated how he had just recovered from his breakdown, how he had just lost all his friends and how he had needed to see a therapist intensely for a month. She was brilliant and Jayden couldn't thank her enough for all the amazing things she had said and done for him.

But he hadn't wanted to do many societies. He had been happy enough when he met Caroline, Kate and Jackie at an Art Social for all the Art students at the university. That had been bad enough.

Jayden hissed as his heart rate increased. His ears rang and he simply forced himself to count out of order. He was still surprised it worked, but apparently the brain couldn't focus on panicking and counting at the same time.

Three women laughed outside and Jayden just grinned as he leapt off his bed and opened it for them.

Jayden was so happy to see Caroline in her thick winter coat (she was always cold even in the height of summer) and Kate in her blue shorts and summer shirt (she was always too hot). And Jayden just hugged Jackie and really liked her sweet coconut perfume.

He felt a little underdressed compared to his friends. He was only wearing blue jeans, black trainers and a black hoody that wasn't even a designer one. Compared to the women that all looked great, wonderful and almost seductive.

"Come on Jayden," Caroline said. "Let's go and see the Societies. There might be that baking one or LGBT+ society you wanted to visit,"

"Watch out Caroline," Kate said grinning. "It might be too cold for you,"

Caroline stuck her tongue out. "No, watch out yourself Kate. It might be too hot for you with all those university students. That's a lot of body heat,"

Jayden smiled. He really had missed his friends.

Jackie hugged Jayden again. "Let's just see if Baking society is on,"

Jayden pretended to roll his eyes out of boredom. There was nothing he would like more than to go to Baking society because he loved cooking. It was so relaxing, fun and the best part was he could eat it.

Jayden was so excited as he left his flat and he was looking forward to putting his past behind him and making new friends. Friends that he wouldn't hurt and friends that wouldn't hurt him almost as badly.

At least he ever had to see anyone from that part of his life again.

Little did know Jayden realise the exact opposite was about to happen.

11

CHAPTER 3
23rd January 2024
Canterbury, England

Zach seriously supposed he should have realised the reason why the Big Fair was called the Big Fair, but it was absolutely massive. He had been in the Sports Hall before and he was always shocked the central hall alone was the size of a football pitch and then there were two other halls that were only slightly smaller than a football pitch on each side.

The Big Fair made use of all the different halls and even some of the small rooms where the University's sports teams met, had their training meetings and teaching stuff.

Zach stood to one side of the massive blue doors to the Sports Hall and he was amazed at the scale of it. He had his back pressed against the perfectly warm green block walls and to his left a river of students washed into the fair.

He had never seen so many students of all

shapes, sizes and ages come together. There were a lot of students in blue, black and even white jeans. A lot of them were designer ones along with the matching designer shirt but Zach didn't mind too much.

Some of the men were seriously hot.

Zach focused on one group of friends in particular as they came in. He couldn't help but focus on their sexy large asses in their black jeans as they stood near him and Lora and decided where to start. They were all wearing designer shirts that highlighted their fit bodies and long black curly hair.

They all looked identical but they were all hot.

"Someone's enjoying themselves," Lora said smiling. "You're grinning like a teenager,"

Zach tried to frown but those men were hot, and it was only now he was realising just how long it had been since he had been out and about and allowed himself to check out men.

He had really missed the feeling.

"What row do you want to start in?" Lora asked.

Zach rolled his eyes as he actually looked for the first time at where the river of students were flowing to. It was a nightmare and there were so many societies to cover.

He realised the Big Fair in the central hall was split out into three rows with different stalls lining each one. Zach couldn't see that much because of the sheer amount of students there but there were things on each stall including swag and other freebies. Zach loved freebies.

There were different things on often for each stall and some of them looked a lot more interesting than others. Like there was marketing society with two large women standing behind it offering people free mugs, but the stall next to it was only offering pens.

Zach still wanted to see both.

"Come on," Lora said.

Zach allowed her to drag him into the massive group of students and they slowly shuffled towards the first row of stalls. He could barely see what the stalls were because there were so many students with the smells of sweat, perfume and manly musk filling the hall. Zach seriously didn't mind the scent of manly musk.

He wanted to roll his eyes because he was only realising now how long it had truly been since he had allowed himself to focus on men. And men were beautiful people.

Zach gently guided Lora forward through a small gap between two different friendship groups, who in their divine wisdom, had just decided to stand in the middle of the row making it hard for others to get round them.

He hated people like that.

Zach pushed Lora forward and they glided through a large group of students until he accidentally found himself at the University Football Society. Zach just grinned like a schoolboy at the rich aroma of manly musk and sweat as he looked at the blue and black football kit the three striking men were wearing behind the little bench.

Zach had no idea why the men felt the need to wear their "used" kit to get new members, but he was hardly complaining.

The man with the words "Team Captain" on the front of his football shirt smiled. "You're Zach, right?"

"Yeah," Zach said wanting to take a step back but he couldn't because of the wall of students behind him.

"I'm Colin. I'm Ryan's new boyfriend. I've heard a lot about you. Do you want to join?"

The words struck Zach like bullets and stab wounds and the entire world just fell away from him. He could see Colin's lips move and he didn't doubt other people were talking about him but he just couldn't hear a word.

This couldn't be happening. He had wanted to move on from Ryan and that part of his life. He couldn't be doing this. He didn't want to be reminded of Ryan and what he had lost.

Zach shook his head and pushed his way through the other students and when his hearing returned he simply kept on gliding through the crowd.

"Talk to me," Lora said.

Zach shook his head and he was glad when he spotted the Baking Society up ahead. He could just focus on that, he was safe and he could deal with

Colin and Ryan later on. Right now he could pretend he was fine and nothing bad was happening.

"Excuse me please," Zach said as he made his way through the crowd with Lora close behind him.

After a few moments of passing art students in long red, colourful dresses, he found himself right next to the Baking stall and he was so happy it was filled with little samples of cookies.

Exactly what he needed after that awful encounter.

"So how much is it for the rest of the year?" Jayden asked.

Zach looked to see who was standing right next to him and as much as he wanted to frown or panic, he couldn't believe he was standing right next to the most striking, stunning man he had ever met.

But also the man that had damaged, hurt and wrecked him because of an innocent mistake.

17

CHAPTER 4
23rd January 2024

Canterbury, England

Jayden flat out couldn't believe how packed the Big Fair was as he went into the Sports Hall. He had never been interested in Sports, he actually hated them but the hall was massive. He supposed it could have been the size of a football pitch but he had no idea what the size of them were. It was an expression that he fully intended to use.

He followed Jackie, Caroline and Katie around through the sea of students up and down the long rows of little stalls. He had wanted to make a little more progress than they currently were but there were simply too many students in all their different clothes, ages and heights walking about.

Jayden rolled his eyes as Caroline pulled them all towards a little wooden table where the Knitting Society (of all things) had set up shop. He had never ever seen the point in knitting, because it was something that old ladies did and Caroline was not an old lady.

But the stall looked nice enough. There were all sorts of red, purple and blue balls of wool on the wooden table. Jayden didn't like the look of the long grey knitting needles but he supposed he could have positioned them in a way that would make the moment come alive.

The vivid colours of the wool mixed with the Sports Hall lighting (which wasn't actually that bad) and the monotone knitting needles were all things he could work with. Jayden nodded to himself because he would have really liked to do that.

The rich, fruity, citrus smells of oranges, lime and lemons filled the stall as a group of young women in tank tops, skirts and little tiny handbags came over. Jayden wanted to cough but he forced himself not too, he didn't want to be rude.

But that aroma was way too strong for his liking.

"And if I knit something how warm would that keep me?" Caroline asked. "The problem is I am always cold,"

Jayden just laughed, because he really did love Caroline as a friend. She was hopeless, always concerned about keeping warm and she was just funny.

Jayden looked at some of the other stalls but it was hard with the wall of other students in his way. He could see a football Society on the other side and Jayden shook his head.

He couldn't imagine him playing football or any sport to be honest. He loved masculine and sporty men but he wasn't into it himself. It was just so damn pointless grown men running around after a ball for 90 minutes. What was the point? They were going to get tired and sweaty and it just didn't achieve anything. Sure it might have been entertaining for some people but to Jayden it was just so, so pointless.

"Oh Jayden," Kate said. "There's baking society over there. Come on,"

"But I haven't finished with knitting Society," Caroline said.

Jayden shrugged. "Join us when you're done, because I have a feeling Katie's getting hot just looking and thinking about wool,"

"Awh you do get me," Katie said giving Jayden a mocking hug and a kiss on the cheek.

Jayden gently took his best friend's hand and they fought through the immense crowd of students. This crowd all mainly seemed to be made up of hot fit sporty men in tight jeans, shirts and their aftershave was so overwhelming with hints of aromantic apple and rose that Jayden was rather turned-on.

Jayden made his way over to the Baking Society stall that was a lot busier than he expected. He stood to one side as the two smiling, clearly happy women in their blue t-shirts were talking to a bunch of other students.

The stall itself was great and Jayden so badly

wanted to help himself to the different samples of chocolate, vanilla and maybe chilli cookies that were on the wooden table. There were pictures of the society's events, their social media details and Jayden had to admit this all looked great.

He couldn't help but smile to himself because he felt like him joining baking society might be a good idea. It would be fun, he would get to meet people and he would get to do tons of fun stuff in the long-term.

The other students moved away and Jayden went with Katie over to the two women who looked really happy to see them. Jayden noticed there was someone else standing next to him, a blond man, but Jayden didn't pay him any attention even though the smell was very familiar.

And very nice.

"So how much is the society for the rest of the year?" Jayden asked.

Out of the corner of his eye he noticed the blond man had turned to look at him and Jayden turned to see who the hell this blond man was.

Fucking hell. He was stunning and he was the man that Jayden had hurt so, so badly.

Jayden's heart pounded in his chest. His chest felt like it was going to explode. His ears rang.

Cold sweat ran down his back. His mouth turned dry. His stomach filled with butterflies and churned and then it felt like an angry cat was inside his stomach.

And then he realise Zach really was beautiful and so damn attractive and striking. He looked as great now as he had back in July and August.

Jayden really loved how Zach was still so insanely fit, sexy and his black t-shirt highlighted how Zach didn't have any body fat, he was so lean and toned without having any muscles. His face was still so perfect and lovely to look at, with his slightly pointy chin, his light blue eyes and his smooth perfect skin. Yet Jayden was so glad Zach was still a hot, seductive blond with his hair parted to the right so it covered his forehead and Zach just looked so strikingly masculine and perfect.

Zach moved a little on the spot and Jayden realised that was the smell he had missed. There was always the subtle smell of manly musk about Zach that had always turned on and made him horny around Zach, but he had fallen in love (toxic love but love nonetheless) in August not because of Zach's perfectly seductive twink body, but because he was one of the nicest people Jayden had ever met.

Now he just needed to know if Zach was still angry at him for all the damage he had caused.

DAMAGE, HEALING, LOVE

CHAPTER 5
23rd January 2024

Canterbury, England

As much as Zach wanted to say, believe and shout that it was bad seeing Jayden again, he just couldn't. He didn't really know what it was but as his heart rate calmed down and some of the dryness of his mouth went away, he realised that Jayden was still a really good-looking guy.

He might not have had much brown hair but his cute face was all lines and angles and Zach had always liked Jayden's deep hazelnut eyes. They were so alert, so full of life and Jayden had always looked at him in a really caring way. Zach had always liked that about him because they both cared so much about each other last August.

Zach couldn't help but smile as he subtly checked out Jayden's rather fit body again. Zach didn't mind that he had some meat on his bones as his mother used to say but Jayden was still fit, cute and he looked so good.

It was only then that Zach realised he had sort of

wanted this chance to meet again. Sure they had seen each other around campus, they had walked past each other and Jayden had tried to say hello. But Zach always stayed silent and kept on walking because he wasn't sure what he would say.

He certainly didn't know what he was meant to say now. He didn't know what Jayden was like, if he had changed or anything. Zach didn't want to talk to Jayden if he was still the same intense, obsessive and overwhelming person he had been in August.

Zach shook at the idea. He couldn't go back but he wanted to see if Jayden was okay, and it wouldn't be a bad thing to see if this cute man was okay.

"How are you?" Jayden asked.

Zach forced himself to take a deep breath and he got an interesting hint of some kind of aromantic apple and rose aftershave.

"Let's go," Lora said pulling at Zach's arm a little.

Zach pulled away from her touch because he was a grown man and he did want to talk to cute Jayden.

"How are you?" Zach asked knowing full well he was dodging the question.

"Yeah I'm good thanks, a lot has changed since August. Therapy went really well, I've met a lot of new friends and life is great. I came out to my parents and my wider family and everyone has been so nice at home,"

Zach just grinned and forced himself not to hug Jayden. That was amazing news that he had come out to his family, it was all Zach had ever wanted for him because Jayden was such a nice guy and his family had taken such a toll on his mental health that it was brilliant to know Jayden had changed.

Zach frowned a little. He was surprised more than anything else because the last time he had seen Jayden, the idea of coming out to his family had been awful, like a death sentence so it must had taken a hell of lot of courage to do that.

"That's brilliant. I am so please for you," Zach said. "I hope things continue to go well and yeah,"

Jayden looked like he was about to reply when a large group of students slightly knocked into him. Zach went to moan at them but he forced himself not to. Jayden wasn't his friend anymore and Jayden could look after himself.

"Thanks, that really does mean a lot coming from you. I know it was something that you always wanted for me, so I'm really glad I did it. How about you? How's Ryan?"

Zach frowned. Jayden didn't know, he didn't know anything because that was how Zach had done their last messages and the ending of their relationship. He had blocked and partly ghosted Jayden on Instagram because it was better for everyone that way.

Zach couldn't believe Jayden didn't know the pain, the trouble and the consequences he had caused Ryan when he had messaged him to find out more about dealing with bad family members. Zach knew it

DAMAGE, HEALING, LOVE

was all his fault because he had told Jayden about Ryan's family when they started to be friends back in July, he hadn't realised Jayden would actually ask Ryan about it. Not that Zach told him it was an off-limit subject.

Zach had seriously screwed up.

"Me and Ryan broke up," Zach said forcing the fakest smile he had ever done. "It was for the best and yeah, Ryan has a new boyfriend after only two months,"

"Who's this?" a woman asked in a t-shirt and shorts.

Zach was a little annoyed that someone would interrupt him and Jayden, but over the sheer deafening noise of the other students he supposed that was bound to happen at some point.

"This is Zach," Jayden said, "and Zach, this is my new friend Katie,"

"Oh *that* Zach,"

Zach felt really cold all of a sudden and he had no idea what he wanted to do, he wanted to run, hide and just scream a little.

"What do you mean *that* Zach?" Zach asked wanting to know.

"Um, just that you hurt him and you wrecked Jayden," Katie said.

"No," Jayden said the panic clear in his voice. "Honestly I only told them at I hurt you badly and what happened between us is why I struggle with friendships,"

Zach shook his head. "I have to go. I have a thing. It was good seeing you and I'm glad you're okay,"

Before cute Jayden could say another word Zach went away and glided through all the different students again with Lora close behind him. He was annoyed with himself because as much as he didn't know how to handle the idea that Jayden had told others about what had happened, he only wanted to spend more and more time with Jayden.

He was so cute, so pretty and so fit but Zach just felt like there was more to it than that. He just had no idea why.

No idea at all.

29

CHAPTER 6

23rd January 2024

Canterbury, England

"I'm sorry Jayden,"

Jayden just waved Katie silent as they all sat around the little white chipboard table in Katie's university kitchen. He certainly didn't like Katie's cheaper accommodation compared to his own because the kitchen was rather awful. It was so small and clinical with its dirty white walls, white cabinets and white kitchen table that was so clearly made of chipboard that it just looked so cheap.

Jayden didn't like to be a snob but it was the truth. There nothing luxurious or even that nice about the kitchen and it was even worse that some of Katie's flatmates had left a small takeaway container filled with mash potatoes, a steak and gravy. Yet judging by the cracked surface of the gravy, it had been uncovered for ages and that was just disgusting.

The only thing Jayden did like about the kitchen

was the fact that Katie, Caroline and Jackie were with him. They all had their bags of freebies and swag arranged on the table, and some of it looked really cool.

Jayden was so impressed that Caroline had gotten a whole bunch of free knitwear including a blue scarf, two red jumpers and some green gloves. She was wearing the scarf now and like always she complained that she was too cold.

Maybe Jackie had gotten the most useful freebies and swag at the Big Fair, because Jayden really liked the three mugs she had "borrowed" from different stalls, and the pens, notepads and other free things were impressive.

Katie had managed to grab some freebies but there was barely anything. And Jayden didn't have anything.

After what had happened with Zach and Katie's wonderful little bombshell, Jayden had sort of walked around the Big Fair like a zombie. He felt so numb, so cold and so emotionless that he didn't know what to feel.

Katie passed Jayden a piping hot mug of coffee, and Jayden really liked the bitter, rich aromas that hit his nose.

"You've told us the story in various ways," Jackie said, "but what actually happened between you, Zach and Ryan?"

Jayden laughed. "God that really is a story and a half but I think I need to tell you,"

"Definitely," all three women said leaning closer like this was the start of a child's story time.

"So I first met Zach about a year ago, he was fucking beautiful and he stood out to me immediately. He was cute, funny and he was just amazing with his blond hair. And we spoke a little but we didn't really do anything else because we didn't really talk, talk,"

"Okay that sounds fine so far," Katie said fanning herself like she was still too hot.

Jayden nodded. "Then back in May we got talking a lot more, we exchanged information on Instagram and then May to July we spoke a fair bit. We made each other laugh, smile and we spoke about Ryan, his boyfriend. It was the start of a good friendship,"

"Okay," Jackie said a little tense.

"Then in July, Zach messaged me saying how he wanted to meet up so we went out. And over the course of the next four weeks we developed a very fast, very caring and very intense friendship. Like we loved spending time together, but I developed a problem,"

"You fell in love?" Caroline asked wrapping her arms around herself because she was still cold. "And you mentioned before you developed Emotional Dependency on him?"

"Exactly," Jayden said, "because my family was so bad towards me being gay and Jayden accepted me without question, I sort of *needed* him to feel loved, safe and secure in myself so that made our friendship very toxic in the end. But he always wanted to support me no matter what happened and no matter how intense I got,"

"He did care about you," Katie said.

"Absolutely," Jayden said. "Like Zach is one of the most caring people I have ever met and he is amazing. And honestly… I did love him truly because he was everything I wanted in a man,"

Jayden didn't like it how his friends didn't look convinced and he couldn't blame them at all. He knew how it sounded, he knew it sounded like he didn't love Zach he was only using Zach for his validation and had a minor obsession with Zach.

An obsession he did not have any more.

"So you had an intense and toxic friendship," Caroline said, "so what broke it?"

Jayden laughed nervously and he just focused on his coffee mug.

"Oh this is going to be good," Caroline said.

"Well," Jayden said, "the problem was I met Ryan. I had been wanting to meet Ryan for ages because I knew Zach really loved him and I honestly wanted to see a gay relationship. But seeing Zach so happy, so in love and so great with someone else, that in itself didn't bother me. But what scared me was the fact that I didn't believe I could ever have that happiness,"

"Why not?" Jackie asked.

"Because of my past and my family. I just didn't think I could have that level of happiness so I just sort of spiralled from there. I was so scared of losing Zach that I tried to become friends with Ryan, but I was way too intense. And I asked him about his own family, the family they don't talk too anymore,"

"And you upset him," Caroline said rubbing her hands together to keep warm.

"Yeah because then Zach messaged me that he didn't want to be friends anymore. Zach was wrong to have shared something so personal and delicate about Ryan's life without his permission and I was being too intense,"

"And that's what led to your breakdown," Katie said not asking but knowing.

Jayden nodded and he took a large sip of the wonderfully bitter and rich coffee.

"How are you feeling now after seeing and talking to Zach again?" Katie asked.

Jayden was about to answer when his phone buzzed and he realised he had a message on Instagram.

Zach had messaged him and that both scared and excited Jayden a lot more than he ever wanted to admit.

CHAPTER 7
23rd January 2024

Canterbury, England

Zach didn't exactly know why he had contacted Jayden but as he looked at his phone just waiting for that annoyingly cute man to reply, he couldn't help but feel so excited and also a little nervous. It was clear that Jayden had changed, he was healthier and he wasn't as intense or needy when they had spoken earlier, but Zach really didn't want to rush into anything.

Zach laid on Lora's bright pink bed, that looked rather horrible in a way, as him and Lora watched a comedy film she raved about. Zach didn't exactly see the appeal and given how much time he had spent in this flat over the past four months, he supposed he should have been used to it by now.

But he looked over to her little desk and there was a wide rack of shelves above it, and there was a row of three large teddies that somehow managed to look elegant and rather adult. Zach just didn't like the one in the middle with the dark eyes that felt like it was staring into his soul.

It was so off-putting.

Lora moved around on the bed and Zach looked up at her as she was laughing, smiling and really enjoying the comedy. She had pulled her long blond hair up into a pony tail and he so badly wanted to talk about today with her, but she had shared her feelings earlier.

She wasn't happy and she did nothing but berate, talk and just complain about Jayden. He understood why she had done it because she had seen how badly Jayden had hurt Ryan and him and their relationship, but the thing was Jayden was never a bad person. He was just really traumatised and he didn't know how things worked and he struggled a lot with friends. Especially gay ones.

It was why Zach had put up with Jayden for so long, but he always felt great, happy and light around Jayden because Jayden was a great guy. And he was so sweet and nice, but it was intense at times.

"Who are you texting?" Lora asked as she stopped the film as it ended.

Zach smiled because he really couldn't tell her that he was messaging Jayden. She wouldn't like that and he would never hear the end of it.

He had only sent Jayden, a message of *Hi, it was nice seeing you today. I'm glad your life's getting better.*

It wasn't too nice, leading or anything it was just

a matter of facts. A good healthy way to start a conversation.

Zach smiled as Jayden replied. *Yes, it was nice seeing you today and life is really good thanks. My friends are nice. What you up to?*

Zach took a deep breath of the creamy pumpkin-spiced latte aroma with a rich splash of vanilla and toffee filled Lora's flat. He almost panicked at the idea of maybe Jayden was being intense again, but he was being silly. It was normal to ask people what they're up to.

Zach texted back. *Nothing much. Just watching a comedy with Lora. What about you?*

He was surprised he actually didn't want Jayden to text back saying that he was with a boyfriend or something. And Zach just rolled his eyes as his stomach filled with butterflies, it was annoying as hell he was finding Jayden cute, fit and he couldn't stop thinking about Jayden's sweet eyes that were so full of life.

"Who are you texting?" Lora asked coming over.

Zach hid his phone so she couldn't look, and he just knew he was going to have to lie to her. Not because he wanted to but because he wanted to save himself from an evening of being told "don't you remember how much he hurt you and you're making a massive mistake,"

"I'm texting a guy," Zach said, "and it hurt like hell knowing that Ryan's moved on and dating someone like Colin, so I wanted to meet someone,"

Lora folded her arms. "And you just happened to have someone ready to talk to just like that,"

Zach nodded like he was a player and he had a million hot sexy men he could contact for some fun at the drop of a pin.

"Of course, I am very hot according to a lot of men," Zach said, "and why do you care so much?"

Lora went over to her desk and took a long sip of her latte. "Because I don't want you contacting Jayden. He hurt you and it was awful seeing you go through that,"

Zach nodded but he didn't like it. When him and Jayden had gone out a few times, Jayden had talked a lot about how his mother and family controlled who he could see and whatnot, apparently Jayden's parents thought the two of them were dating for those months.

An idea that made Zach smile, because Jayden was a cute, caring guy that just wanted the best for the people in his life. Zach supposed it wouldn't be a terrible idea to see about dating, but he had to know Jayden was different before he committed to anything.

He was not going back to the way things were in August. Lora was right, that was hell for him too.

"I'm not talking to Jayden because you're right. He really hurt me, he caused me and Ryan to break up by mistake and he just isn't the right guy for me," Zach said knowing he was lying because he actually wanted to meet up with Jayden so badly.

"Okay good," Lora said. "I'm going to the kitchen. Do you want anything?"

"No thanks," Zach said looking back at his phone.

I'm in my friend's kitchen talking about what happened today. I did like seeing you and I am sorry about Ryan. He was a great guy.

Zach couldn't help but smile. Jayden was always so sweet, so caring and such a great guy.

It's okay. Zach said not knowing if that was true or not. *I'm actually curious to see how much you're changed and um, what else you've been up to lately. Want to hang out sometime?*

As soon as Zach hit send he couldn't believe what the hell he had just done. He wanted this badly and it would be good if him and Jayden could be friends again and maybe even boyfriends, but he was nervous. Jayden was amazingly sweet but he could be so intense with his feelings. Zach didn't want to hurt him and he really didn't want Jayden to hurt him in return.

Sure I'm busy for the next few days with lectures and assignments but Saturday sounds good.

Zach was shocked and grinned like a schoolboy. The old Jayden would have said something like *any time is great* or Jayden would imply that he was prepared to drop everything he was doing or had planned to spend time with Zach.

But he wasn't like that anymore, Jayden was actually going to wait four days to see him.

And that was brilliant and Zach was so excited about Saturday. It could be brilliant or it could be awful.

42

CHAPTER 8
27th January 2024
Canterbury, England

Jayden flat out couldn't believe how brilliant, wonderful and lovely it had been just talking to Zach over the past few days. They hadn't spoken for very long or very deeply but it was nice just talking about university and whatnot. Jayden was glad that Zach was enjoying his course, he had made a bunch of friends that he sometimes hung out with and he was thinking about joining the Fencing Society.

Jayden seriously couldn't have cared less about Fencing or any sort of sports, but he couldn't deny the idea of Zach wearing sportswear was a massive turn-on. It would be good to see Zach's fit, sexy body without a gram of body fat covered in sportswear. Jayden just grinned to himself.

He was sitting on a rather cold wooden chair inside of one of the university's many little cafes and restaurants that were spread out all over campus.

Jayden rather liked this one because it was sort of an Italian joint with its warm cream colours, little photographs of Italy and the wonderful aromas of basil, tomatoes and garlic filled the café.

It was brilliant.

Jayden rested his arms on the slightly cold plastic table and really wanted Zach to hurry up so they could see each other. There were a lot of other students in the café because it was lunchtime and most of them were having a working lunch.

The table in front of Jayden was filled with a group of young women in hoodies, jeans and they all had their laptops out. Some of them had yellow legal pads and they were debating some kind of group project that at least two of the women hated with a passion. A rather cute waiter went over to them with a tray full of pizza and that managed to make the two women smile a lot more.

Jayden smiled weakly at the waiter as he went pass and he looked at his own half-empty cup of coffee. The Italians (even fake ones like this café) really did know how to do great coffee with just the right amounts of sugar, milk and bitterness that left a good aftertaste on the tongue.

"Hey," Zach said.

Jayden looked over and just grinned like a little schoolboy as the most beautiful man he had ever seen came over to him. Zach looked so striking in his black t-shirt that highlighted how fit he was, how he didn't have any muscles but he was so lean and fit and

Jayden just wanted to hug him. And Zach's thin legs looked good in his black jeans and he was so stunningly perfect.

"Hi," Jayden said as he watched Zach take a seat and they sort of looked at each other and smiled.

Jayden had really missed Zach's smile because he was so cute and attractive when he did smile.

"I have no idea where to start," Jayden said. "All I know is a lot has happened and I respect you enough to let you decide what you want,"

Jayden was a bit surprised that Zach looked a little shocked. He supposed it was fair considering part of emotional dependency and Jayden making their friendship toxic was he had made it very one-sided by mistake. So maybe Zach was surprised he wanted a more equal one.

"Oh okay," Zach said. "Well hey, I contacted you because I want to see what happened to you and how your life is now, because I did care about you a lot. And I think I might still care about you but I don't know,"

"Okay, let's see how today goes and *you* can decide if you want a friendship or not and we can go really slow," Jayden said.

He was actually rather impressed with himself, because he had played out this situation a thousand times over the past few months in his head. Like what would he say or do if Zach ever wanted to get back together as friends and hopefully more now that he wasn't with Ryan.

And in some of the situations in his head, Jayden was sadly intense and said his feelings too soon, but he hadn't today. Something he was so glad about.

"Katie seems nice, how did you meet?"

Jayden laughed because that was sort of connected to his breakdown, so that was going to be interesting for sure.

"So after you and me stopped being friends and after everything I did to get you back, I realised I needed more friends,"

"More friends besides me," Zach said smiling.

Jayden was glad Zach felt comfortable enough to make a small dig in his wonderfully caring voice that Jayden had missed.

"Yeah, because my breakdown was about gay stuff and my abuse and trauma. I found a little social club for gay young adults, like you said I should find, and that's how I met Katie. She's bi,"

"That's great and I'm glad you did take onboard what I said. That's why I told you and gave you those resources,"

Jayden really liked just talking, reconnecting and spending some time with such an attractive, fit and stunning man. And Jayden was surprised he wasn't anxious, scared and his ears weren't ringing like he had always expected them to if he had seen Zach again.

"Want to order some food?" Zach asked.

Jayden had been waiting for him to ask that because he wanted today to last as long as possible but he couldn't say it. Because the key to building a friendship first and maybe a relationship was to go slowly and that was exactly what Jayden intended to do.

Little did Jayden realise just how large the difference between *intending* and *doing* actually was and messing up that difference had massive consequences.

CHAPTER 9
27th January 2024

Canterbury, England

Zach had been in this particular café plenty of times with Ryan and Lora and some of their other friends, and he had always liked it. The chefs here did the best pizza ever because it was so fresh, so flavourful and the pesto here was to die for. Zach was really glad he had suggested it because after an hour of talking, laughing and smiling about everything and nothing, he was realising why he had been friends with Jayden in the first place.

Zach watched as Jayden finished off his pasta dish with a name he wasn't even going to try to pronounce. It looked cheesy and really nice with chunks of tomatoes, basil and little bowtie pasta shapes. Zach's own dish of Neapolitan pizza had been really delicious with the rich, creamy cheese, rich garlicy tomato sauce and the little touch of basil at the end was a nice touch.

Zach just couldn't believe he was enjoying his time with Jayden so much. He had always been interesting, he had always been caring and he had always been such a nice, wonderful guy that Zach was sort of expecting he was into him a lot more than he wanted to admit.

"Do you mind if I ask you a question about Ryan?" Jayden asked.

Zach froze for a moment so he wrapped his hands round his pint glass of diet coke so it looked like he had been thinking about if he wanted a drink or not.

"Sure," Zach said really not wanting this question to ruin their lunch together.

"What happened? And please know how sorry, so sorry I am for what I did to him," Jayden said.

Zach smiled a little. That was typical Jayden being caring enough to say sorry even though he didn't really know what had happened. Zach had never revealed how much Jayden's question had hurt his ex-boyfriend. Zach had just stopped talking to Jayden before anything else could happen.

Something he was starting to regret.

"What happened?" Jayden asked in a caring and slightly seductive tone that surprised Zach.

Zach was about to answer when a group of students behind him with yellow legal pads started arguing about something. And they had packed up and thankfully left.

That was why Zach hated group projects.

"When you asked Ryan about how he dealt with his parents and family, you freaked him out. It was even worse that you told him I told you about that so he shouted, screamed and he was so mad at me," Zach said.

Zach focused on the bubbles in his Diet Coke as he talked. He didn't want to look at cute Jayden, this was his fault and he should have handled everything better.

"I tried to explain that I had told you a month before and I didn't even expect you to remember. I certainly didn't remember telling you and then he was so mad at me. He actually stayed with Lora for two weeks,"

"Oh shit," Jayden said. "Then what happened because I started to try to get you back after three weeks,"

Zach sighed. He actually wasn't sure what was the worst bit about August and the very early chunk of September. When Jayden had asked the question that had been the first chip in Zach's and Ryan's relationship, or the messages and even a letter trying to get Zach back as his friend.

Zach wasn't sure but that was an intense time.

Zach smiled as he got a whiff of a waiter's apple and rose aftershave with a slight undertone of musk.

"It was okay to be honest for the first week after he came back. We had a lot of sex, he smelt amazing as always with his manly musk and it was nice. Then you started to try to get me back, I tried to hide everything about that from him but he found your letter,"

Zach looked up and he hated seeing how pained Jayden was as he placed his face in his hands with only his sweet eyes visible.

"It was a nice letter by the way, a little long but it was nice hearing what had happened in therapy and why you were the way you were," Zach said.

"But I was silly and intense trying to get you back,"

Zach nodded. "Then me and Ryan had another fight because, I know you are such a cute and nice person. I know you are capable of caring about people so much and you don't know how to process those feelings at times,"

Jayden nodded.

"But Ryan and Lora and everyone doesn't believe me when I say how nice you are and how… I just like you for a reason I don't know or even understand. I just want to be your friend," Zach said.

Zach realised that might have been a little forward but he was really enjoying having lunch with Jayden, a great, cute, attractive man that cared about him. And he had clearly changed for the better.

"I would like to be friends again," Jayden said.

Zach made himself look away for a moment and he focused on the long line of lecturers in their business suits, white shirts and black shoes near the counter. He wanted to be friends again with this cutie.

Zach nodded. "Okay great. But remember, go

slow. We're different people now, you're cute and let's just keep things slow for now,"

"Of course," Jayden said. "But you find me cute?"

Zach just grinned and shook his head because he couldn't confirm that. He found Jayden really cute, attractive and he wanted to do some things to Jayden but he had to protect himself first.

He wanted things to go slow but Zach couldn't deny he wasn't sure he could wait that long. And that was a feeling he hadn't had for a long long time. Maybe since him and Ryan had first met all those long great years ago.

CHAPTER 10
8th February 2024

Canterbury, England

Jayden had absolutely loved the past two weeks with sexy, fit Zach because they had been texting every single day for at least an hour talking about their day, what had happened in the past and just normal friend stuff. Jayden had loved talking with his old best friend and it sort of felt like this was a lot better and healthier than it had been before.

And he flat out loved how light, wonderful and cared for Zach made him feel, but Jayden couldn't deny he was scared as hell about making a mistake. He was always double-checking his messages because he just couldn't afford to sound too intense, too invested and too damaged to Zach.

He couldn't do that again.

"Pass me the eggs please," Caroline said.

Jayden grabbed the six-pack of large eggs on the black chipboard kitchen table that was in Jackie's block of flats. He had never been here before but he rather liked it. The kitchen was massive and Jayden had no idea how many people shared this kitchen, it had to be at least ten or twelve, and everything was black.

Jayden rather liked the smooth black cabinets that were almost posh for university accommodation, the black oven hummed a little louder than he would have liked but he wasn't too concerned, and the bright yellow lights in the ceiling lit up everything perfectly.

The only bad thing about his own flat kitchen was how the lights flickered from time to time. It wasn't meant to but Jayden was just glad modern phones had a torch on them.

He liked the sweet aroma of vanilla, chocolate and mixed spice that filled the kitchen from the cookies and cakes they were baking. He had no idea how the conversation had popped up at first, but he was cooking and that was what he loved doing. Well, he loved it now the girls had strong-armed him into helping out.

"How many cookies are we making?" Jayden asked mixing his own bowl of butter, sugar and flour together.

"I don't know. The University Sports Collective want people to help fundraise for new kit so we are helping," Jackie said.

"It is a little cold in here, don't you think?" Caroline asked adding some vanilla extract to her bowl.

"No, if anything it is way too hot with these ovens on," Katie said.

Jayden just laughed. He had actually been missing his friends lately because instead of spending most evenings with them, he had been texting Zach and he had been working on a bunch of art assignments. He was so glad his drawing was getting better.

"So how's it going with Zach?" Caroline asked readjusting her knitted scarf.

"Really good thanks, but I am a little scared. You know how bad I am with friendships," Jayden said.

"Rubbish," Katie said. "Just because your first friendship with Zach ended in a rather impressive way doesn't mean you're bad at friendships,"

"Sure you can be intense at times," Jackie said. "But we learnt how you work and you learnt how we worked in turn and we love having you as a friend,"

Jayden nodded and he finished mixing up his ingredients and added some mixed spice. He flat out loved the great, rich depth of flavour the brown powder gave his cookies.

He couldn't disagree with his friends though. They were right and he had almost had a fight with Caroline and Katie in the first two months of their friendship because they had accused him of being too intense. And Jayden had argued that he was only being nice, something they agreed to in theory but all the *nice* things Jayden said came out as way too intense.

To the point he made them uncomfortable.

"Why don't you just talk to Zach about your fears?" Katie asked fanning herself with a baking tray.

"Because that's scary and we've only been talking again for another three weeks. It was about this time I started the series of unfortunate events that fucked us up the first time," Jayden said.

He mixed his bowl a little more as his heart rate increased, sweat poured down his back and his ears started ringing.

He forced himself to quietly count out of order but he was tense. He didn't like that fact and now he was just scared he was going to mess everything up like last time.

"Jayden? You okay?" Jackie asked.

Jayden nodded but he was lying. He was not okay. All he wanted in the entire world was to be with, talk to and hug and kiss sexy Zach, but he couldn't. It didn't matter how much he seriously liked Zach, they just couldn't be together because he would mess it up and hurt Zach again and again.

Something he simply could never ever allow.

CHAPTER 11
9th February 2024

Canterbury, England

As much as Zach flat out didn't want to admit it, he couldn't get the idea of Jayden covered in flour, mixed spice and other sweeter things had out of his head. He had no idea he was turned on by the idea of Jayden cooking, but he just wanted to see Jayden again.

And Zach was so impressed that Jayden really had changed because 99% of their messages and conversations were fine. Of course some of Jayden's messages were borderline intense, like how much Jayden cared about him considering they had only reconnected three weeks ago but it was milder than they used to be.

"When am I going to meet your boyfriend?" Lora asked.

Zach laughed to himself as him and Lora went into the bread isle of their local supermarket. He had never been to this one before but it seemed okay, the prices were good, the staff were all fit young men including two Zach had slept with, and the food looked good.

The current isle had a rather interesting (tasteless) black and white diamond tile pattern on it, and the left hand side was lined with some great artisan breads, some commercial ones and some pastries. Zach so badly wanted to buy tons of croissants. They looked great.

Yet Zach was way more interested in the right hand side filled with cakes, cupcakes and an entire range of delicious, creamy, sweet coffee cakes.

"I thought you would like the coffee cakes," Lora said.

Zach stood in front of them and studied them. They looked amazing and the rich aromas of yeast, freshly baked bread and buttery pastries hit his nose, and Zach just knew he was going to be spending a lot of money in this one isle.

"Your new boyfriend when do I get to meet him," Lora said like a child.

"Soon and I think you'll really like him," Zach said.

He wasn't exactly happy he had been lying to Lora for weeks about him texting Jayden, and the one time they had gone out. Yet Jayden was so cute, so funny and just so careful. All Zach wanted to do was look into his strikingly sweet blue eyes again.

Jayden was so, so cute and Zach always felt

brilliant around him.

"Why don't you just tell me who it is?" Lora asked picking up a commercial coffee cake.

"Because I don't want you to scare him off. You're very intense in your protection of me," Zach said knowing the irony there.

"That's only because you let some traumatised loser in your life, he wrecked it and caused you to lose the best relationship you ever had,"

Zach subtly looked at Lora and bit his lip. That wasn't fair, that wasn't right and she was wrong. Jayden was not a loser, he was not a traumatised wreck and he did not ruin anything.

Zach wasn't even sure that Ryan was the love of his life anymore. Sure Ryan was amazing, beautiful and just a God amongst men but he wasn't Jayden. Jayden was so sweet, so caring and so intimate in the non-sexual ways that he didn't actually believe for a moment Ryan was capable of the same.

"Don't you agree?" Lora asked pointing to a more artisan coffee cake.

Zach picked up the smaller but more decorative coffee cake filled with caramelised coated walnuts, and he didn't doubt it was going to bite him in the ass, because this wasn't how he felt but he nodded.

"Yes Jayden did ruin a lot of stuff in my life but he isn't a bad person," Zach said glad he didn't have to lie about the last part.

Lora laughed. "I love you as a friend Zach and I will always protect you,"

Zach smiled his thanks to her and he placed the artisan coffee cake in Lora's basket and they moved onto the bread section. He wasn't exactly a massive fan of bread but he liked sandwiches so they were a necessary evil.

He was really impressed as he looked at the rows upon rows of white, brown and seeded loaves that covered the shelves. It was going to be a nightmare to choose.

"Why don't you like Jayden though?" Zach asked. "Like I know he hurt me so badly and he wrecked Ryan too, but is there anything else?"

"Yeah," Lora said. "I met him once and he's a nice guy but he's just… I don't know. He's pathetic. Like if your life really is as bad as he made out to you then why didn't he fix it sooner?"

Zach tensed a little. That was not a fair question and that was something he always liked about straight people that had lived perfect lives. Lora was a classic straight girl who had had good relationships, had a perfectly supportive family and had never ever been told that being straight was wrong.

Zach hated it how it was pointless trying to tell her about homophobia and how tough life and families could be for queer people. She just believed that because she was really supportive that everyone else was too.

So he went with a classic line that he knew was wasted breath.

"You can only help yourself when you're ready

and you might find me ending the friendship with Jayden gave him the kick he needed to change," Zach said.

"Maybe but he should have done it sooner,"

Zach didn't even comment as he picked up two large packs of croissants and him and Lora went to the checkout.

As much as he loved Lora as a friend, he just wanted to be with Jayden so he was going to invite him out today for a little light lunch.

And that excited Zach way more than he ever wanted to admit.

Little did he realise things were about to start changing. Some good. Some bad.

DAMAGE, HEALING, LOVE

CHAPTER 12
11th February 2024

Canterbury, England

Jayden was so excited that sexy, attractive, fit Zach had asked him out again for a little bit of lunch. He really didn't care what it was, he was just glad to be getting another chance to spend time with him, because texting was great but he just wanted to be with him.

Jayden had to admit as he sat down on the little wooden picnic table that had certainly seen better days (some of the wood had rotten away around the edges) that a picnic lunch might not have been the best idea for February. It was wet, a little chilly and damp.

It might have been right next to a narrow road with a few red, black and green cars parked on one side, but it was private and small. Which Jayden really liked, he loved these small private moments with the man he was falling for, and he never wanted to stop having these moments.

Jayden shivered a little as he got comfortable on the bench of the picnic table but he just couldn't stop looking at Zach as he sat down with a little white tote bag filled with food. Jayden still couldn't believe how artful, fit and divine he looked, and how perfect his body was even with Zach wearing a thin little blue coat.

"Do you remember when we last did this?" Zach asked.

Jayden laughed. "Yeah, me and you were talking one day and Ryan had gone to visit a friend up North so you wanted something to do. And then you of all people convinced me to go painting. I haven't touched watercolours since,"

"You were good though," Zach said getting out a whole host of different picnic pieces.

Jayden smiled to himself. He really liked the croissants, vegan sandwiches, little chocolate eclairs and other things that Zach had brought. It was going to take a while for them to finish this, which was hardly a problem because that just meant he got to spend even more time with the man he was seriously falling for.

"Do you still paint much? And didn't you do puzzles or something?" Jayden asked knowing the answer was yes.

Zach's face lit up and Jayden loved seeing his beautiful, perfect smile that reached all the way up to his eyes.

"Of course, I really like doing puzzles and now I'm back at my uni flat I can spread out on the kitchen table. I have this really beautiful one at the moment that's sort of an abstract photo with stunning, bright colours,"

Jayden reached over and picked up a vegan turkey and stuffing sandwich. He really liked knowing that Zach was still doing what he enjoyed, he was still passionate and he was still excited about a lot of things. And it was so great to hear him talk about his hobbies.

"I would like to see it at some point," Jayden said.

Then he bit his lip because he realised what he was basically asking. He was asking Zach to come to his apartment block, where he lived, studied and slept and that might be a little too soon.

"Relax," Zach said going for Jayden's hand but stopping himself.

Jayden smiled because he so badly wanted Zach to touch him, hold his hand and for something more to happen. And it was a little weird that Zach had gone to touch him, even during their first friendship Zach had never ever done that before.

It was strange and Jayden realised that Zach might actually like him a little more than a friend. It might explain why both of them had been texting each other every single day without fail, and there was interest on both sides. He was wanting to know the ins and outs of Zach's day and Zach would want to know the same for him.

But it was time to stop being a little too cautious.

"Do you like me?" Jayden asked.

His heart pounded in his chest. He didn't want this to be the fuck up moment again. He couldn't keep fucking up friends around the three-week mark.

Zach grinned. "What do you mean *like*? As a friend or more,"

"More," Jayden said.

Zach grabbed a vegan ham and cheese sandwich and Jayden opened his sandwich and he seriously enjoyed the rich, spicy aromas of the vegan turkey and the stuffing that he just knew would be an incredible explosion of flavour on the tongue.

"I think… I think yes I might be into you romantically," Zach said, "because you do make me feel good, I know you're really caring and I have never thought you're a bad guy,"

Jayden didn't know how to take the last part because he wasn't a bad person. He never had been and never ever would be.

"Do you like me?" Zach asked grinning.

"You know I do. I never spoke to you about it when we were friends because you were with Ryan and I respected the hell out of that relationship,"

"And that's why I like you," Zach said liking how Jayden respected his past relationship, "because you're so caring, you're so good and you are really nice,"

Jayden took out the sandwich, surprised by how

incredibly soft the white bread was in his hand.

"So," Jayden said, "do you want to try us dating?"

"Aren't we already?" Zach asked grinning. "We text daily, we go out and we both like each other's company,"

"Maybe we are," Jayden said but he so badly wanted to say so much more and he couldn't believe how brilliant this lunch was.

All he wanted to do was hug, kiss and hold Zach's hand, but he forced himself not to. Zach had only agreed to date and this was the start of a new relationship. They had technically only been dating ten seconds, but Jayden felt like he had been dating and being with Zach in his mind for weeks.

Jayden was about to say something when he saw someone out of the corner of his eye.

"What the hell are you two doing?" Ryan asked.

Jayden's stomach churned up a storm as he realised his nice peaceful lunch was going to end badly.

69

CHAPTER 13
11th February 2024

Canterbury, England

Zach flat out didn't understand what was happening as he watched Ryan with his sensational body storm over to him and Jayden as they sat at the picnic table. He had picked this spot at the university because it was isolated, private and perfect for a date in all but name.

Zach just looked at how great Ryan looked with his sensational biceps, six-pack abs and insanely fit body as his tight-fitting black hoody and jeans left little to the imagination.

"What the hell are you two doing?" Ryan asked.

Zach didn't need this. He had only wanted to have a nice lunch with a friend who he really, really liked. He didn't want any drama, any pain or trouble, and he certainly didn't want to see his ex-boyfriend.

He placed the vegan ham and cheese sandwich back in the packet because as much as he wanted to enjoy the extreme creaminess of the cheese, he simply had to deal with this first.

"We're having lunch together and it isn't any of your business who I spend time with," Zach said knowing it was a complete and utter lie because of who Jayden was.

Ryan stopped right next to Zach and Zach forced himself not to smile as Ryan's thick manly musk hit his nose and made his wayward parts spring to life. Ryan must have just finished football practice or something so he would be hot, sweaty and horny as always.

"Do you not know what *that* boy did to me? To us? He is a hurtful, self-fish, intense idiot. They are your words, not mine and you are spending time with him," Ryan said.

Zach didn't dare look at Jayden. He didn't know what he would say because Ryan was right, he had said a lot of nasty stuff about Jayden in the weeks after he had ended their friendship.

"And how long has this been happening? And most importantly why the hell would you let that loser back into your life after what he did to you, to me and our relationship? Did you ever end the friendship?"

Zach just looked straight into Ryan's eyes. "Of course I bloody did. I ended my friendship with him, because he was too intense, he was a nightmare and he was toxic back then. He's better now and healthier,"

Ryan laughed and looked at Jayden. Zach had no

idea what either one of them were thinking, he wanted to spare Jayden some pain and make up some half-truth about what had happened behind closed doors but he couldn't.

Ryan wanted to have this fight and he was going to have it now of all times.

"You called you every word under the sun you know," Ryan said grinning. "You called you pathetic, weak, a wreck and everything else. He doesn't care about you. You're a charity case, a nothing and you never will be anything,"

Zach was about to say something when Ryan walked away and Zach found some strength to stand up.

"You ended you and me you know. And I only started talking to Jayden three weeks ago. That's the truth,"

He never had expected Ryan to turn around and respond but it still hurt that he didn't. Zach had never wanted to hurt anyone and Ryan had been a great boyfriend who cared and treasured Zach a lot, but Zach couldn't really understand why Ryan had never forgiven Zach for telling Jayden things about his life.

Zach could understand the things he had told Jayden in an effort to help him were never his things to share, but that wasn't a reason to hate him for months and then dump him. Not after Zach had done a million things to make it up to him.

"Are you okay?" Jayden asked.

Zach laughed as he looked at the cute, innocent

man that he had always cared so much about. It was why he had listened and allowed Jayden to basically shit all over him about his mental health, how bad his life was and how bad his family was.

Because Zach really, really cared about Jayden. He was so cute, so sweet and so perfect in every way and even now, Jayden was still focusing on others.

He was so amazing.

"No not really," Zach said. "I didn't want to hurt Ryan and I didn't want to hurt you,"

Jayden gestured he wanted to reach across the table and hold Zach's hand, which Zach allowed. They both grinned like schoolboys as they enjoyed the warmth, attraction and sexual chemistry that flowed between them.

Zach gently rubbed Jayden's hand. "I am sorry you know about what I said,"

Jayden tensed. "You didn't have to confirm it,"

"I didn't want to lie to you. It all mattered but I was so angry and mad at myself, Ryan and what had happened to our relationship that… I regret a lot of things I said about you,"

"Do you still think of me like that?"

"Never," Zach said picking up his ham and cheese sandwich again. "I like you a lot so let's try to move on. Let's focus on the future, do you want that?"

"I really would," Jayden said as he finished off his own sandwich and moaned in pleasure at the taste.

Zach just hoped beyond hope Jayden would one

day moan at him in utter pleasure because he loved that sound and he really wanted to hear it over and over again.

CHAPTER 14
11th February 2024

Canterbury, England

As much as Jayden didn't want to admit it, he couldn't help but have Ryan's cold, hard words replay constantly in his head. He was helping Caroline (who was now wearing three scarves because it was apparently too damn cold), Jackie and Katie (who was wearing blue shorts and a tank top because it was too warm on an icy cold February late afternoon).

Jayden really didn't understand his friends' temperature sensitivities at times, but he loved them, supported them and considering he had ditched them to hang out with Zach, he sort of owed them.

Jayden had two large plastic boxes filled with about a hundred largeish chocolate chip cookies. The rich butter, sugar and dark chocolate hints that filled his senses made Jayden really want to chomp into the box himself, but Jackie had made a plate of cookies for the four of them so sadly he was going to have to wait.

Even though he seriously didn't want to.

Jayden really liked the main plaza of the campus, where the Sports Guild wanted everyone to leave their donations. Jayden had always liked how large it was so three rows of exotic food trucks could line up and serve students. Today it seemed like the local Indian, Chinese and Japanese food trucks dominated the scene.

Jayden had always preferred when the middle eastern trucks were there but hopefully they would be back tomorrow or sometime soon.

"What is that smell?" Caroline asked loudly.

Jayden laughed as he looked over to the coffee shop next to university bookshop with beautiful, breath-taking displays of the latest bestsellers and the local corner shop on the very end.

He coughed a few times as the coffee shop had clearly burnt their coffee beans yet again. It was so overwhelming, so awful and so strange that Jayden was definitely going to get out of here as soon as possible.

"That coffee shop's always burning their bean," Jackie said as she carried three boxes of cookies.

Jayden followed the women as they all made their way towards the large white tent in the middle of the plaza with a long line of students with their own donations.

Something he had no intention of waiting for.

"Hey," Katie said, "didn't you say you saw Ryan

earlier?"

"Yeah why?" Jayden asked.

"Isn't that his boyfriend Colin?" Katie asked gesturing with her head to the white tent.

Jayden just rolled his eyes and frowned. Of course it was bloody Colin up ahead taking all the donations, writing up what was what and smiling and being all friendly when in reality he was a dickhead.

Zach had only told him what had happened at the Big Fair about a week into them restarting their friendships. Jayden had wanted to say some strong words but he behaved himself.

He flat out couldn't believe that Colin would actually shoved the fact he was Ryan's new boyfriend in Zach's face. Who did that? Especially considering how much Zach had been hurting at the time.

"You alright?" Caroline asked.

Jayden smiled at her. "I don't know,"

And then Jayden told them all about what Ryan had said to him about Zach's choice words when their friendship had ended.

"He was angry," Jackie said flicking the plastic boxes up because they were clearly getting too heavy for her.

"I guess so but if he really cared about me back then, why would he say it?" Jayden asked.

"Dearest," Caroline said shivering slightly, "you know how much we love you but you ever think, you and Zach are living too much in the past,"

Jayden shrugged. He had no idea what the hell

she was talking about, but Jayden couldn't help himself when he realised how great the light was with the cold grey sky above with but small rays of golden sunlight still managed to light up the sky.

It was only now Jayden was realising just how much he had been neglecting his passion, his favourite hobby and the thing that had gotten him through so much. He definitely needed to go on an "artist date" again to just take photos.

And enjoy his favourite artform.

Jayden stepped out the way of a student as a large group of them walked past.

"Answer the question," Jackie said smiling.

"I don't know Jackie," Jayden said. "You have no idea what it was like to have a breakdown, lose someone who you had a toxic and very unhealthy relationship with and then have to recover from that,"

The women went silent and then Caroline wrapped her scarves a little tighter and smiled.

"I'm sorry, we don't know what it was like," Caroline said. "We only know the aftermath and how much you struggled during those four months when you were trying to get back on your feet,"

"But," Jackie said, "we also know how great you are, how caring you are and how much Zach means to you now. Maybe just see if you can let go of the past, hurt and anything that happened between you both,"

Jayden smiled. "If I wasn't holding these boxes I would hug you all,"

"Then let's put down our boxes," Katie said.

Jayden put down his boxes at the same time his friends did and then they all did a massive group hug, because they were right. He should talk to Zach about just forgetting and not worrying about the past.

They were different people now and he was healthier, stronger and he wasn't dependent or intense with Zach anymore. He knew what to say and what not to say to people.

And the very idea of that made Jayden so damn excited because it meant there could be a real wonderful, lovely chance of him and Zach having a relationship that was healthy and not wrapped up in the past.

A past that was extremely hurtful and damaging for both of them.

Little did Jayden realise everything was about to come crashing down.

CHAPTER 15
17th February 2024

Canterbury, England

Now Zach definitely knew how Jayden had felt when he had asked him out that one time to do painting in the woods where both of them lived, the idea of an "artist date" sounded silly, a little weird and a little woo-woo. But if it meant spending time with someone as fit, hot and attractive as Jayden then he was up for it.

Which was probably the exact same reason Jayden had agreed to go painting with him.

"This is beautiful and perfect for painting," Jayden said.

Zach just grinned as him and Jayden walked through Blean Wood. The air was cold, damp and crisp so there might not have been much mud but the ground was lumpy and uneven. Not that Zach minded too much.

He had always wanted to go to Blean Woods

near Kent University but he had never had the time to go yet. And now he was here with the man he was seriously falling for, he was so damn happy that he had come here.

Zach was rather impressed with the thin silver birch, pine and oak trees that lined the pathway. Their branches were shooting out in all directions and long blanche vines hung off some of the trees.

"Oh wow. That is so perfect," Jayden said as he knelt down, messed around with angling his professional camera and he took a few shots.

Zach laughed, because Jayden was so damn cute. He had no idea what Jayden saw in the Woods, it was a complete mystery to him but he loved, truly loved seeing Jayden so happy and in his element.

When Jayden came over to him and showed him some of his photos, Zach was amazed at how detailed the photos of a Robin were in the trees. The detail in the photo was only amplified by the lighting, the slight sparkle on the branch because of the frost being hit by the sunlight at just the right angle.

"You're amazing you know," Zach said.

Jayden grinned. "Um, I really want to kiss you,"

Zach smiled and he honestly couldn't have cared less that he was technically in public and Jayden had said back in August that he would never kiss another man in public.

Zach took a step closer and he gently stroked Jayden's cheek with one hand and he ran the other hand down his black coat.

He liked it when Jayden's breath caught and Zach went closer.

When their lips met, Zach moaned in pleasure as Jayden did the same. The kiss was electric, intense and so tender and filled with so much passion that Zach never ever wanted this kiss to end.

This was so much better than anything Ryan had ever given him because this was a deep, intense, caring kiss. It wasn't a hot, I-want-to-fuck-you kiss, this was a you-matter-so-much-to-me kiss.

And Zach loved it.

"Wow," Jayden said. "Thank you,"

Zach playfully hit him on the arm and he took Jayden's hand in his as they went along the pathway. Whilst trying not to twist an ankle on the uneven ground.

"You know when I see something picture worthy I'm going to let go," Jayden said grinning.

Zach ignored it. "You don't have to thank me for kissing you. I like you a lot and, I meant what I said about wanting to give us a try now you're better and healthier,"

Jayden looked around. "Thanks, and you know I am so sorry for what happened before,"

"I know," Zach said meaning it. "You were just trying to deal with a bad situation at home, you were trying to do it all alone and you just developed an unhealthy attachment to me because I was the only person that accepted you,"

"And you're beautiful," Jayden said.

"Getting intense again," Zach said with a small smile.

"Sorry," Jayden said as he let go and knelt down to take another photo of something in the trees.

"See but I like this, this is what we need to do. Just be open, talk and just you make a mistake I'll correct you and you can do the same with me,"

"Now that I would like. Definitely going to make talking to you less stressful for me," Jayden said.

"And that's what boyfriends are for,"

Zach stopped dead in his tracks as soon as the words left his mouth. The term *boyfriend* felt strange, awkward and a little weird to say out loud. He had called Ryan his boyfriend for more years than he cared to admit so it felt a little weird calling Jayden of all people his boyfriend.

But he couldn't help but smile because it felt good, right and lovely to call him his boyfriend.

"One of my friends mentioned something a few days ago," Jayden said. "She thinks both of us are living too much in the past,"

Zach nodded and he jogged a little to catch up with Jayden who was already taking more photos of something up ahead.

He supposed that was sort of fair. Both of them had been concerned about how the other would react because of what had happened before, so maybe they should forget the past and just live in the moment. And if something connected to the past popped up then they would deal with it.

So that's exactly what Zach told him.

Jayden hugged him and Zach liked the feeling of his hard body against his.

"Actually," Jayden said. "When we went painting that time I really wanted a photo of us together. Can I… I don't know, have one now?"

"Sure but how can you take a selfie on that pro cam of yours. Does it have a secret selfie setting?" Zach asked failing to stop himself from laughing.

Jayden playfully hit Zach on the head. "No I have a phone for that,"

Zach went over to Jayden and they both placed a tight, caring arm around each other, they grinned and they both took some pictures.

Zach poked his tongue out on some of them. They both pulled silly faces and then there were nice ones and happy ones and photos that just made Zach want to cry in happiness. He loved this. He loved these small precious moments where they could be a real couple without worrying what others would say about them.

Lora was still banging on about how he was hiding something and Ryan had been messaging him on social media. Ryan was threatening him, telling him he was making a big mistake and Zach had tried blocking him but Ryan just had a new account.

"Want to think about going back?" Jayden asked after they took a final couple's photo together. "It's early, we can catch a film or something at my flat,"

Zach laughed and he was about to respond when

he heard a twig snap in the distance.

"Seriously!" Lora shouted. "This is your boyfriend. What the fuck!"

Zach's eyes widened as he realised shit was about to hit the fan.

CHAPTER 16
17th February 2024

Canterbury, England

Jayden flat out couldn't believe what was happening here. It couldn't be her, not Lora. Anything but that woman with her long angelic blond hair that had made his life hell back in September and October when he had seen her a few times.

Not Lora. She was evil, harsh and an awful person who hated him.

Jayden felt his heart pound in his chest, cold sweat ran back down his back and his ears rang slightly as he watched as her and Ryan come down the path towards them. The uneven frozen ground didn't even seem to slow them or bother them in the slightest.

The pine, oaks and silver birches moved slightly and their branches banged into each other as an icy cold breeze flew through the woodlands. And Jayden just knew that this was going to end badly.

"So this is your boyfriend?" Lora asked frowning.

"I wasn't lying to you," Zach said. "I just sort of bent the truth because Jayden wasn't my boyfriend when we first started talking,"

"How bloody long has this been happening?" Lora asked.

Jayden shivered at the rage and anger and hate in her voice. He hadn't realised Lora still had so much hate in her after she had cornered him in one of the shops on campus and really bit into him.

Jayden had cried so damn much that evening and he had done everything he could to forget it.

Ryan stepped forward. "See Lora Zach doesn't care about you. You were always a good friend to me after what that loser did to me and Zach, but Zach just doesn't care. He only ever thinks of himself,"

"Shut up," Jayden said. "You're a snake and you just hate me for going what you went through,"

"No," Ryan said taking a few steps closer to him. "I hate you because you are a loser, a charity case and you are nothing,"

Jayden forced back the tears. It was happening all over again but instead of happening over text, it was happening to his face.

"Enough," Zach said. "Me and Jayden are trying to date and I was going to tell you and-"

"He's only going to hurt you or have you actually forgotten what that loser did to you and Ryan back in August?" Lora asked.

Jayden couldn't help but look at Zach. He had

always known he had hurt Zach with his intensity, his obsessiveness and his sharp questions about how to cope with his trauma and abuse but he had never wanted to know *just* how much he had hurt him.

The man he seriously liked and cared for and maybe even loved.

The dampness in the air got even thicker as Jayden realised that Zach was looking at the ground. He might have been thinking or remembering and Jayden really wanted to support him.

Surely that was how good relationships were formed, one partner supporting the other partner and then their relationship got even stronger and better. That was how it worked, surely?

Jayden took a few steps forward. "You might not like me but I do love Zach and I genuinely care about him. I won't hurt him again and I'm better now,"

"No you aren't," Zach said looking up at Jayden with watery eyes.

Lora and Ryan laughed and Jayden shivered as he hated the sound of that cackling.

"You have only known me again for three weeks. You can't *love* me," Zach said straining to keep back the tears. "You are so intense, so connected to feelings that it takes others time to develop and you... you are so lovely but I can't keep doing this. Every time you come into my life you cause so much upheaval,"

Jayden's eyes widened. It was happening. He had fucked-up yet again because he had been too intense, he had said those little words too soon and Zach didn't feel the same.

He was an idiot.

"So… so you're siding with them?" Jayden asked pointing to Lora and Ryan.

Zach shook his head. "You all pretend to care about me but Lora you just want to control me. You could have asked and respected my decision to talk to Jayden again. And Ryan stop texting and threatening me,"

Jayden was about to say something and question that but Zach just glared at him.

"You are so caring and kind but, I just can't keep doing this with you," Zach said as he walked away.

Jayden looked at Ryan and Lora as they looked all nice and smug and Jayden stood his ground. He didn't need to be scared of them anymore, he didn't need to be concerned about what they thought of him, he didn't even like them.

When Zach was out of sight Ryan and Lora smiled and bowed and walked away.

"Loser," Ryan said.

Lora turned around. "And you do realise, it was only a week ago Zach said *Jayden ruined a lot of stuff in my life*,"

Jayden didn't dare react until they were out of sight and then he simply fell against an icy cold oak tree and he let everything out.

All his pain. All his anger. All his sadness.

It all came out.

CHAPTER 17
17th February 2024

Canterbury, England

Zach had absolutely no idea if it had been forecasted to rain later in the day but he hadn't checked. He continued along a long road filled with potholes and wonderful little semi-detached houses with white exteriors, perfectly clean driveways and little rose gardens out front as he went back towards the university.

The rain fell down all around him and Zach just smiled for a moment because his coat was thin, so it was good for warmth in the cold but it was useless in the rain. Especially heavy rain like this one.

A black car drove past him with its headlights on as the grey sky started to turn a little black. Even three of the streetlamps turned on as Zach went past because it was so dark like his mood.

Zach was slightly regretting finding a park bench to sit down for a long time (he had no idea how long he had sat there just hating his life and hating everything about Ryan) because now he was caught in the rain and he was going to get soaked.

Zach was surprised how deafening the rain was as it splashed onto the pavement, it hit tin roofs of little outbuildings in people's gardens and cars past him.

This really wasn't how he had wanted today to go but he had sort of always known this was what would happen in the end.

He had always known that Jayden "loved" him and Zach wanted to joke to himself that it was impossible not to. Jayden had always liked blonds and men with fit bodies and Zach supposed he was very good in both departments.

He had just never wanted Jayden to be so intense in that particular moment. Not when Ryan and Lora were there with him or against him as was the case. Zach had really wanted Jayden to be quiet and maybe he could have reasoned with his friend and ex so they would leave him alone.

Zach shivered as his hair was soaking wet, his coat wasn't doing anything anymore to keep the water out and the light cold breeze was starting to chill him. He still had another five, ten minutes easily before he reached the university and then another ten minutes of walking before he reached his shared flat.

It wasn't ideal but nothing about today was.

Zach couldn't really blame Jayden though because he knew he had only been trying to help.

Jayden was probably trying to be the same lovely, caring and wonderful person that he always had been. He probably saw the situation with Lora and Ryan as a problem that needed to be fixed and he wanted to try.

He was great like that.

Zach smiled to himself as he kept walking through the rain because he really did like Jayden.

Zach had never really meant something as kind, caring and great as Jayden. Because sure Jayden could be intense as hell at times, it was wrong of him to say he loved Zach after only three weeks, but Jayden had never been a bad person.

And Zach wasn't sure he wanted a repeat of the past.

He had never really given it much thought before now because he had been so focused on Ryan and angry at Jayden. But it had sort of killed him the first time he had put his friendship on pause with Jayden.

He wasn't sure why he felt like someone had ripped out a part of him, but now he supposed it was because Jayden had been such a good, lovely and fun friend for that month.

They had talked a lot, gone out a lot and they were always smiling and laughing and having fun. And Zach had hated putting the friendship on pause because that meant all the "fun" just stopped immediately.

He regretted that now.

Zach shivered again as the rain came down even

harder and he was fairly sure he looked like a drowned rat with his blond hair being darkened and awful.

He was so cold and shaking. He just wanted to go home back to his apartment.

Zach tried to get his phone now so he could text one of his flatmates to put the kettle on and make sure the heating in the shared kitchen was on, that radiator was bigger so he could dry more of his clothes, but his hands were shaking too badly to do anything.

He was so cold.

Zach saw a large white SUV drive up next to him before it sped up and drove right through a puddle.

It splashed all over him and Zach just wanted to cry. This day wasn't going right but he wasn't going to let the past repeat itself.

He cared and seriously liked Jayden so he was going to go to his shared university accommodation and get warm there and sort this out.

Mainly because he didn't want to lose Jayden but also because Jayden's accommodation was so much closer than his own.

And right now he only wanted to get warm and he seriously wanted to get warm in Jayden's arms.

CHAPTER 18
17th February 2024
Canterbury, England

Jayden was rather impressed with himself for not spending any more than twenty minutes crying, screaming and just being angry at himself, the world and Lora (with Ryan just being a natural idiot). He was even happier he had managed to make it back to his university accommodation before the rain had started.

"I hope Caroline doesn't melt out there," Katie said fanning herself.

Jayden smiled to himself as he wrapped his hands round the piping hot mug of coffee that Jackie had made him.

They were all sitting in Jayden's shared kitchen and Jayden was just glad it was so clean for a change. He had never seen the black fake-marble countertops so clean, shiny and they smelt of orange-scented bleach. That wasn't a bad smell at all. Jayden was

DAMAGE, HEALING, LOVE

impressed the other flatmates had really been brilliant about their cleaning responsibilities after the university had moaned and officially warned them yesterday.

Even the black chipboard dining table that had more cracks and holes than most UK roads was rather impressive. Jayden could almost see his own reflection in it but Jayden seriously doubted Caroline would melt.

"She isn't a witch you know," Jayden said.

"How do you know? She's always cold and the rain only makes things colder," Katie said grinning. "Maybe she's cold blooded,"

Jayden almost jumped at the deafening sound of the rain hammering into the glass windows of the kitchen that was only amplified by the echoing in the kitchen. He really hoped the rain would lighten up soon.

Jackie took a few sips of her herbal tea and shook her head.

"I'm sorry about what happened," Jackie said before looking at Katie. "Because someone here needs to be supportive,"

"I was going to comfort him but I was more concerned about Caroline and I hate this heating by the way,"

Jayden smiled. He really did love his friends.

"Do you think you'll contact him again?" Jackie asked like how a mother might ask a small child something.

97

Jayden shrugged. "Yeah probably, but not for a few days. Part of the reason why Zach put our friendship on pause in the first time was because I was contacting Ryan too much in an effort to become friends with him,"

Katie went round the table and hugged Jayden. "I am so proud of you,"

"Why?" Jayden asked.

Jackie looked like it was obvious. "Because that's healthy. It means you can learn from your mistakes and you want to get better at friendships and relationships,"

Jayden nodded. That was fair and he really wanted Zach to know he was different, he was healthy and he was committed to trying to be a good boyfriend.

"But how are you doing?" Katie asked taking a seat at the table.

"I don't know to be honest. It was so… weird seeing Lora again because I hadn't seen her since the start of the year,"

"What happened and why didn't you tell us?" Katie asked. "You've known us all since September,"

Jayden just looked at his steaming coffee. "Because after everything with Zach I convinced myself that talking about how I was wasn't a good thing. I didn't want to burden you and our friendships were way too new for that sort of information,"

Katie looked like she was going to say something but Jackie just glared at her.

"Maybe you're right and me and Katie don't have to think about the same things as you when it comes to friendships,"

Katie nodded like that was what she had always wanted to say.

Jayden was about to say something because he felt great and he had always liked how wonderful Zach made him feel, but the rain got even louder and he could barely hear himself think over the noise of the rain against the window.

Then it went quiet for a moment before the rain continued to hammer down and echo around the kitchen.

"I miss him," Jayden said. "I really miss Zach and I don't want him to be angry with me. I didn't mean to hurt him, and don't, want him to go through what he went through in August,"

Jackie and Katie smiled like they knew something.

Jayden took a sip of his strong bitter coffee and gestured them to say whatever they wanted, he really hoped it was going to be helpful.

"Then you wait a few days, prove you aren't intense and obsessive like before and then you fight for this relationship," Jackie said. "You go slow to continue to prove how much better you are and then you convince Zach through your actions that this relationship matters,"

Jayden nodded. He liked the idea of that because all he wanted in the entire world was to see Zach's fit, sexy body again and amazing smile. Jayden wanted to kiss Zach's soft, wonderful lips again and he really wanted to run his fingers through Zach's delightfully soft blond hair.

Zach was so beautiful and perfect and Jayden's stomach filled with butterflies.

He got what he said was wrong and he shouldn't have said he loved Zach so soon, but he really, really did.

The kitchen door opened and Jayden's mouth dropped and he couldn't help but grin as Caroline came in (soaking wet) with some blond man that looked like a drowned rat.

The most beautiful drowned rat Jayden had ever seen.

CHAPTER 19
17th February 2024
Canterbury, England

Zach was so damn cold and he couldn't stop his shivering as he stood in the doorway to Jayden's shared kitchen. He was glad Jayden had mentioned where to find his flat and accommodation in passing in a random conversation they had been having over text, because he was so damn cold.

He really liked it how Jayden came over to him and hugged him and gently pulled himself inside. Zach just grinned because he knew that Jayden was going to take good care of him and then when he was thawed out Zach really hoped they could sort everything out.

As Jayden focused on getting him out of his soaking wet coat, Zach wanted to cough at the sheer strength of the cloves, oranges and lemon aromas in the air. Maybe it was from bleach or something because the kitchen was so clean but it was strong.

Too strong for it to be normal.

The sheer strength of the aromas made Zach's eyes water and his body kept shivering. He had never seen countertops so shiny and clean and black, and the dining table that looked like it was going to fall apart at any moment looked relatively new (from a secondhand store).

"Tea or coffee?" the woman who called herself Caroline asked.

Zach tried to talk but his teeth were chattering too much. He hated being this cold and wet but he loved it when Jayden hugged him tight after putting his coat on the radiator near the window.

Zach hugged Jayden as tight as he could manage as he shook. And he realised if someone walked past they might have thought he was twerking on Jayden, he was shivering so badly.

Zach gasped as Jayden playfully put his wonderfully warm hands under Zach's wet hoody and he grinned like a little schoolboy. He was even happier that Jayden didn't stop and Zach laughed and his wayward parts sprung to life as Jayden explored his body.

"I knew you were fit but I didn't realise you had such a hard body," Jayden said like he was a kid in a candy store.

"Here's your coffee," Caroline said clearly choosing Zach's drink for herself.

Zach clung to Jayden a little as they went over to the dining table with two other women already sitting around it. He had no idea why one of the women were wearing shorts and a tank top on such a cold day so she had to be Katie.

"Are you okay enough to come into my room and change?" Jayden asked. "Just to get you into some new clothes, I promise I can wait outside whilst you change and we don't have to talk or anything until you go back,"

Zach rubbed his hands together and he wrapped them round his wonderfully warm coffee mug. He smiled at Jayden for a moment because Lora was so wrong about Jayden. He had changed, he was different and he was a lot more aware of his intensity at times.

Of course Jayden would make mistakes but Zach knew he wasn't exactly perfect either. But he still wanted him and Jayden to work out so that was why he was here.

"I appreciate it you know," Zach said grinning. "It means a lot that you're trying but I wouldn't mind getting out of my clothes, and you can watch if you want,"

Zach was so glad he was sitting down as his wayward parts were showing as clear as day to see in his soaking wet jeans.

"I wouldn't mind that either," Jayden said as they both got up, took their mugs with them and they both said bye to the girls.

Zach followed Jayden out along a narrow little corridor with dirty white walls and the same blue carpet squares that the university seemed to be obsessed with.

Then Jayden opened a door and they went into his flat. Zach was impressed with it, it was rather lovely, small but lovely. He smiled at the rather beautiful photos hanging on the walls, he knew he shouldn't have been but he was always surprised at how great of a photographer Jayden was.

The bed was small, a little high and Zach wasn't sure if he was going to have to jump up to get on it, but that was definitely a theory to test later on.

Jayden pushed past him to get to a small wardrobe and Zach watched as Jayden expertly picked out a matching black outfit of a black hoody, jogging bottoms and a black t-shirt. Zach had wanted to ask for some boxer briefs so he could get out of his soaking wet underwear but he supposed he wanted to keep Jayden guessing about some stuff in their relationship.

"Here you go," Jayden said weakly smiling as he passed the clothes to Zach. "I am sorry you know,"

Zach nodded. "I know you are and that's why I'm here. Stand over there, watch me get changed if you want and we'll talk because I think there's a lot we need to fix before we can be together,"

"Like what?" Jayden asked, "you make it sound like there's more to fix than you and me,"

Zach nodded because as much as he didn't want to admit it, he did want his best friend back.

"I know it sounds stupid but Lora is a great

friend and she cares about me a lot. If there's a chance we can still be friends and if she can accept you're a good part of my life then I want to take it. Is that okay?"

Zach wasn't sure what Jayden was going to say for a moment but after a few seconds, he nodded.

"If that helps you to be happy then that's okay and we all need more friends these days,"

Zach hugged him. Jayden really was brilliant, caring and wonderful and he was so glad he had come here to fix everything.

Now he just needed to get out of these soaking clothes and get warm.

107

CHAPTER 20
17th February 2024
Canterbury, England

Jayden had absolutely no idea what he needed to do in this situation as he leant against a warm white wall of his flat. He watched a very hot, fit and soaking wet Zach place the clothes down on his bed and Zach stood in the narrow gap between his desk and his bed.

Jayden had always wanted to see Zach's fit, attractive and just divine body under his clothes but he had never thought he was actually going to see it. Especially with Zach shaking and shivering so much from the cold.

All Jayden wanted to do was go over to Zach and brush his soaking wet hair to one side and just kiss him and love him.

"You nervous?" Zach asked as he took his drenched hoody and damp t-shirt off.

"Maybe," Jayden said.

Jayden couldn't help but grin like an idiot as he admired Zach's insanely fit body. He had always known there were no muscles and no real definition to Zach's body but it was still amazing to look at. There wasn't an ounce of body fat, Zach had a strong stomach line and his body curved slightly so Jayden was certain if Zach did some ab workouts he would have a six-pack in a short order.

He was that fit.

Jayden was surprised when Zach didn't put on his dry hoody and t-shirt. Instead Zach took off his soaking wet jeans and Jayden gasped in pleasure.

Zach's legs were long, sexy and thin like he had always known. They were hairless and smooth and Jayden really wanted to run a hand up them and Zach's package was hardly a bad side.

And Zach was clearly aroused to say the least.

Then Jayden crossed his own legs as Zach got unchanged into Jayden's favourite black hoody, jogging bottoms and t-shirt.

"That was very nice. Thanks for that," Jayden said.

"You're welcome I want to see your body at some point too,"

Jayden laughed and shook his head because this was why he had always loved him and Zach. Their friendship and relationship was so fun, full of laughter and it was so positive.

"Help me up," Zach said as he tried jumping up on Jayden's bed but he couldn't.

Jayden hugged and lifted up Zach and he accidentally threw him on the bed and then Jayden sat next to him.

"Note to self you throwing me on the bed is hot," Zach said like he was embarrassed.

"So we're okay then?"

"Yeah. I think we always were okay but I was just shocked that you said *I love you* and there was all the grief from Ryan and Lora and I just needed some space,"

Jayden took Zach's hand in his. "I know I can be a lot at times and I know the intensity of emotions isn't normal, but I am trying. Just ask the girls because I have been intense with them before and I am a lot better now,"

Zach nodded. "I know, over the past three weeks I know you've been a lot better and not *as* intense. Sure you're going to make mistakes at times because you are intense and that's partly why I like you so much,"

Jayden smiled. His stomach filled with butterflies at the idea of Zach liking him a lot.

"And I know," Zach said, "I can't change how intense you feel things, but I can tell you and help you come across as less intense. Like if we're talking and you get intense then I'll just tell you and we make a course correction or something. Is that okay?"

Jayden nodded and hugged Zach.

"That was all I ever wanted in the first place," Jayden said. "When you put us on pause and when I was trying to get you back, I know I was super intense and maybe even a little unstable back then, but you only had to talk to me."

"Yeah, um sorry,"

"It's okay," Jayden said breaking the hug and running his hand through Zach's damp hair.

"Let's just promise from now on we'll start talking more, we'll focus on being us and supporting each other. Because I want this relationship to work,"

"Me too," Jayden said.

Jayden loved it how Zach pulled him close and kissed him again. Jayden couldn't believe how great and soft and wonderful Zach's lips felt against his and he never wanted this moment to end.

It was perfect.

"You want to watch something and snuggle?" Zach asked.

Jayden nodded and grinned like a schoolboy as he grabbed his laptop and snuggled with the beautiful man he loved.

He knew that they still needed to fix Zach's and Lora's friendship and deal with Ryan but tonight was about them. And that made Jayden a lot more excited than he had been in his entire life.

And that was a great feeling to have.

CHAPTER 21
24th February 2024

Canterbury, England

Zach was flat out shocked that he had to take a leaf out of Jayden's book when it came to Lora, because Zach had wanted to text her, phone her and fix everything about their friendship the day after she had almost wrecked his relationship with the man he loved. But Zach couldn't believe that Jayden had been right that he should wait a few more days, maybe a week and then approach Lora.

Now Zach knew exactly how Jayden felt when he had paused their friendship, even though this was slightly different.

About a week later, Zach held the hand of the beautiful man he loved as they both sat down in the library café at a small plastic table with a horribly wobbly leg, as they saw Lora coming towards them.

The entire café with its white walls, massive floor-to-ceiling windows and tons upon tons of students revising with their friends made Zach smile a little. He had never liked coming to the library café because he just wasn't comfortable and he had always revised better in his room. If he wanted to see his friends he would go out with them, he seriously wouldn't revise or study with them.

"You okay?" Jayden asked.

Zach laughed. "You're always asking about me. Shouldn't I be asking you about how you're feeling, after all Lora did shout at you a few times?"

As much as Zach had loved spending the past week kissing, hugging and watching films with Jayden, he had hated to find out what Lora had done behind his back. Even when he was so annoyed at Jayden for his intensity and emotional dependency, she never should have shouted or cornered him.

That was wrong.

"Thanks for the coffee," Lora said sitting down on the chair opposite them.

Zach smiled at his old best friend. Lora looked really well and she was sipping the coffee they had brought her so she clearly wasn't *that* angry at them.

Zach squeezed Jayden's wonderfully smooth, soft hand a little. He hated Jayden to start talking but Lora was his friend so this was his problem to solve.

"I'm sorry Zach didn't tell you about us," Jayden said. "I never wanted that and I've actually always liked how good you two are as friends,"

Lora took a sip of her coffee. "Thanks because unlike you I don't hurt Zach and I always look out for him,"

"You're hurting me right now," Zach said.

Zach had never expected to say it but he was only realising how he had been spending the past week, and every waking moment with the man he loved, because he didn't want to be alone so he could think about how badly his friend had treated him.

"What do you mean?" Lora asked. "I am only looking out for you, it's what I have always done,"

"You have done nothing but-" Zach said.

"I think you mean that," Jayden said, "but I think you're going about it the wrong way because you are hurting his feelings,"

Zach was surprised Jayden could speak so calmly, nicely and like Lora actually had a good point. Maybe he didn't need to fix this problem alone.

"I think," Jayden said, "you want to know about me and if there is any chance I am going to hurt Zach again like I did before,"

Lora played with her coffee cup and nodded a little. Zach was glad to see she was calmer now with the rich bitter aroma of the coffee filling the air and she leant forward so she had to be listening to Jayden. There was clearly a first time for everything.

"I have been through therapy, I have been through a lot of personal growth with my friends that I have now and I am a lot better. I've dealt with my past really well and I'm dealing with everything that pops up,"

"Okay," Lora said playing with her coffee cup

DAMAGE, HEALING, LOVE

even more making the aroma of coffee even more intense, "but can you promise without a shadow of a doubt you will never hurt him again?"

Zach looked at the man he loved and smiled, because it was a pointless question. They were a couple in love, they liked each other a lot and Zach just knew there might be arguments or intense moments in the future but it didn't matter. They were two people in love and they would deal with everything that popped up.

"I love him," Zach said grinning like a schoolboy, "and that means I'll take the so-called risk,"

Lora frowned. "You can't love him,"

Zach looked at Jayden and he really did love those light blue eyes, they were perfect.

"Why not?" Zach asked. "He's kind, caring and just so great. And honestly, I want to see where this relationship goes, I'm not scared anymore and if you have a problem with that then I don't need you in my life,"

Jayden kissed Zach on the cheek then Zach kissed Jayden on the lips. They might have been kissing for over a week now but Zach still flat out loved how great of a kisser Jayden was. He never ever wanted to stop kissing this beautiful man.

"You know what," Lora said smiling. "If you're happy then I can be happy for you too. I actually haven't liked the past week very much,"

Zach cocked his head. He had spoken to some of

their other friends in his lectures and they had all been spending lots of time with Lora.

"And yes I know I spend a lot of time with the gang at the bar but… they aren't you,"

Zach laughed. "I am pretty great,"

Zach loved hearing Jayden and Lora laugh together and then Zach hugged his best friend.

And for the next three hours, Zach just grinned, laughed and talked with his boyfriend and his best friend for the first time ever. They spoke about their lives, their degrees and everything in-between.

Zach loved every moment of it because it just showed him the power of having honest conversations and standing up for the person he loved.

Now there was only one problem left to deal with and Zach could be with Jayden forever. Something he was definitely looking forward to.

They had to deal with Ryan.

DAMAGE, HEALING, LOVE

CHAPTER 22
26th February 2024
Canterbury, England

Jayden had never expected to like Lora as much as he did but after spending a few hours with her in the library café, texting her a little and meeting with her and his friends this morning, he couldn't deny that she was actually a great woman with a really interesting life.

But this was the moment they had all been planning for the past two days.

Jayden held Zach's wonderfully soft, smooth hand tight with Lora, Caroline and Jackie close behind them (Katie was already at their destination talking with Ryan to stall him from escaping) as they went through the large brown corridors with gym lockers lining the walls as they went towards the main sports hall.

Jayden couldn't help but grin as he could see that Zach was getting a little turned on because of the slight aroma of sweat that filled the corridor. Maybe Ryan's football team had just finished a practice session and Jayden playfully jabbed his boyfriend.

"Relax I am getting distracted," Zach said, "but I might give you a little reward later,"

Jayden's stomach filled with butterflies at the idea of having sex with the man he loved. He would love that.

They all went through the white doors and then hooked a left and then a right through more gym-locker-lined corridors before they made it to the main sports hall.

Jayden was surprised how massive it was without all the stalls and other students inside. The immense football pitch was all marked out, the block walls of the hall were gigantic and the three other people in the hall looked like ants from this distance.

They all went towards the three people. Jayden could see Katie a mile away with her blue tank-top, short-shorts and black fan that she was still fanning herself with. He was never going to understand her.

Jayden's heart started to pound in his chest. his ears rang slightly. His stomach tightened into a painful knot.

He could see Ryan and Colin talking to Katie. They looked annoyed as hell and Jayden really couldn't have anything bad happen, not today, not any day.

"Babe?" Zach asked. "You alright?"

Jayden kept on walking but he smiled as his body

relaxed. He actually was okay, for the first time since August, maybe ever because he truly was okay. He was with his friends, Lora and his boyfriend.

This was everything he had ever wanted and Jayden couldn't believe how great it felt to have friends and a boyfriend that cared, liked and wanted to be with him. He didn't have to panic or be scared about them leaving him because they had all chosen to be friends with him and they liked him for him, and there was no changing that.

Jackie, Caroline and Katie had proved that time and time again, and Jayden had really liked how they had taught him how healthy friendships worked after a few problems. And they were still here today and wanted to help him.

And Zach was still here and loved him and was an amazing boyfriend because... he just was. Jayden was never going to question that because it didn't need to be questioned. Jayden loved him too.

"That wasn't a foul in the last minute!" Colin shouted at Katie.

"Don't you dare shout at her," Jayden said a lot harsher than he normally would.

"Oh my god the loser and the dumbass are still together. And what?" Ryan asked with a massive grin. "Lora, I thought you were better than that, he lied to you,"

Lora shook her head. "You are nothing but a liar that manipulates people to make them miserable,"

Ryan shrugged like that was nothing.

"I might have loved you once," Zach said, "but I will never love you again. I don't even know what I saw in you,"

Jayden smiled even more as Ryan's grin disappeared. Jayden had no idea that would hurt Ryan, maybe Ryan still loved Zach and was only trying to get him back.

"Come on babe let's go," Colin said. "Let's leave these losers alone,"

Ryan shook his head. "But... but I don't understand how *this* happened?"

Jayden laughed as Ryan shook his head around and highlighted how him and Zach were holding hands like a true couple.

"Because," Jayden said, "you will never understand true love. Love doesn't have to be explained, logical or make that much sense. Love is about respect, joy and that strange feeling you have inside you whenever you see that person,"

Jayden so badly wanted to kiss Zach but he didn't want to go out of his way to annoy Ryan. Jayden was annoyed at him, he didn't want to be cruel to the idiot.

"And Jayden's amazing," Caroline said pulling on her knitted scarf.

Ryan frowned and Jayden was surprised when his shoulders slumped forward and he looked really down.

"Babe come on," Colin said starting to walk away.

Ryan took a step towards Zach and everyone except Colin took two steps closer to Zach. Jayden was not letting Ryan anywhere near his boyfriend.

"We really aren't getting back together are we?"

"No," Zach said. "You were lovely once and I think when you aren't being a dick, you might still be lovely. But no I don't love you anymore and I haven't since August. Since I met Jayden here, what he did to you back then was awful and he triggered so much for you. I get that but you could have handled a lot of stuff differently,"

"We all could have," Lora said.

Jayden felt a lump form in his throat.

"Yeah you're right," Ryan said and he looked at Jayden. "I forgive you and I'm really sorry for what you went through,"

"And you," Jayden said stepping forward and hugging Ryan.

When Jayden broke the hug, Ryan gave Zach a little kiss on the cheek for old time's sake and Jayden just grinned as Ryan and Colin walked away hand in hand.

He wasn't really sure why he was smiling so much, or why his stomach filled with a swarm of butterflies or why he felt so damn amazing. But he had a feeling that it was because everything was settled and perfect. He had a wonderful boyfriend that loved him more than anything, he had so many friends that he really liked and they were so much fun to be around, and Ryan wasn't going to bother them anymore.

That was the great thing about dealing with the past. It could be dealt with, overcome and everyone could move on in the end.

And as Jayden kissed Zach's wonderfully soft, full lips again, he had to admit he was the luckiest man in the world. And he couldn't help but appreciate that he had sorted everything out in the sports hall where him and Zach had reconnected and ultimately started their journey of falling in love.

A journey that had to be the best journey in the world.

CHAPTER 23
24th April 2024
Canterbury, England

About two months later, Zach really enjoyed how warm and light the evenings were starting to get now it was April, and it might have been the Easter Break away from the university, but Zach still loved spending every minute of every day with stunning Jayden.

Over the past three months, they had spent every day together and kissed and done more adult things almost as often. Zach really liked hanging out with Jayden alone with all their friends and he didn't even consider Lora his friend or Caroline, Jackie and Katie Jayden's friends anymore.

They were all their friends and he really liked that.

Zach still didn't want to admit how much he was enjoying photography with Jayden, and he was so damn proud of Jayden for starting to sell photos to magazines, on his own online store and he was making good money from it.

And the past three months were the best ones of his life.

"I love you," Jayden said.

Zach brushed Jayden's smooth hair as they both sat on top of the warm grass hill at the university that overlooked the striking city of Canterbury. There were so many treetops standing up like soldiers but beyond that there were tons of ancient rooftops, the Cathedral spire and so many other landmarks showing off Canterbury's impressive history.

Zach had always loved sitting here in the evenings and talking with his friends and past boyfriends, but this time it felt extra special. Him and Jayden had sat here a few times but tonight, it just seemed extra romantic and Zach couldn't deny he was really enjoying stroking Jayden's hair. It was so smooth and nice that Zach didn't want to stop for a while.

"Don't forget we're meeting your parents tomorrow?" Jayden asked.

Zach laughed. He was looking forward to that a lot more than he wanted to admit, because it would be fun. His parents would pretend to be tough and interrogating because they were somewhat aware of what had happened back in August, but Zach knew after the first ten minutes they would love Jayden.

They would be able to see he was happy, in love and Jayden was so much better than Ryan. Zach was still surprised Ryan and Colin were together and Zach had seen them together a few times since they had sorted out everything, and he had to admit, Ryan and Colin looked even better than they did when they were dating.

"What you thinking about?" Jayden asked.

"Oh, nothing much," Zach said grinning. "Just how you and me are a great couple, how much I love you and how much better my life is now I know you,"

Jayden laughed and blew Zach a kiss. Zach playfully ran a hand down Jayden's hot, sexy body and nodded at a group of girls in summer dresses as they walked past.

Zach moved over a little as Jayden sat up and pulled him close.

"You know why tonight feels even more romantic than normal," Jayden said more of a statement than a question, "and we've known each other a long time to be honest,"

Zach nodded. They might have only been friends and dating for a total of six months including their first attempt in August, but Zach felt like he knew everything about Jayden, and Jayden had said the same about him.

"Yeah, we've been through more together in a few months than most couples ever have to deal with," Zach said smiling.

"Exactly," Jayden said taking a small black box out of his pocket. "Zach James will you do me the honour of becoming my husband?"

DAMAGE, HEALING, LOVE

"Yes!" Zach shouted kissing, hugging and making the beautiful man he loved fall backwards onto the grass. Then they rolled over kissing and celebrating the best news in their entire lives.

And that was what happened.

They both went to Zach's parent's house the next day and it was the best time of their lives, because Zach's parents were happy, delighted and they were more enthusiastic about the wedding than they were (something Zach had no idea was possible).

Then 9-months later in the Christmas break from university, they married and Zach flat out loved it, because him and the man he loved more than anything in the entire world were together forever. And neither one of them had a problem with that in the slightest.

And Zach realised on his wedding day that when you truly love someone like how Zach loved Jayden and Jayden loved Zach, it didn't matter who they were before, how bad their life was or their mental health, people could improve, get better and life could be great.

Zach was so proud of Jayden for everything he had accomplished and they had both helped each other be better in ways Zach never thought was possible.

And as Zach and Jayden drove off towards the airport for their honeymoon, Zach felt like the luckiest man alive because him and Jayden had gone through damage, healing and love and that made their love even stronger.

Something Zach would always, always treasure.

DAMAGE, HEALING, LOVE

GET YOUR FREE SHORT STORY NOW!
And get signed up to Connor Whiteley's newsletter to hear about new gripping books, offers and exciting projects. (You'll never be sent spam)
https://www.subscribepage.io/gayromancesignup

About the author:

Connor Whiteley is the author of over 60 books in the sci-fi fantasy, nonfiction psychology and books for writer's genre and he is a Human Branding Speaker and Consultant.

He is a passionate warhammer 40,000 reader, psychology student and author.

Who narrates his own audiobooks and he hosts The Psychology World Podcast.

All whilst studying Psychology at the University of Kent, England.

Also, he was a former Explorer Scout where he gave a speech to the Maltese President in August 2018 and he attended Prince Charles' 70th Birthday Party at Buckingham Palace in May 2018.

Plus, he is a self-confessed coffee lover!

DAMAGE, HEALING, LOVE

Other books by Connor Whiteley:
Bettie English Private Eye Series
A Very Private Woman
The Russian Case
A Very Urgent Matter
A Case Most Personal
Trains, Scots and Private Eyes
The Federation Protects
Cops, Robbers and Private Eyes
Just Ask Bettie English
An Inheritance To Die For
The Death of Graham Adams
Bearing Witness
The Twelve
The Wrong Body
The Assassination Of Bettie English
Wining And Dying
Eight Hours
Uniformed Cabal
A Case Most Christmas

Gay Romance Novellas
Breaking, Nursing, Repairing A Broken Heart
Jacob And Daniel
Fallen For A Lie
Spying And Weddings
Clean Break

Awakening Love
Meeting A Country Man
Loving Prime Minister
Snowed In Love
Never Been Kissed
Love Betrays You

Lord of War Origin Trilogy:
Not Scared Of The Dark
Madness
Burn Them All

Way Of The Odyssey
Odyssey of Rebirth
Convergence of Odysseys

The Fireheart Fantasy Series
Heart of Fire
Heart of Lies
Heart of Prophecy
Heart of Bones
Heart of Fate

City of Assassins (Urban Fantasy)
City of Death
City of Martyrs
City of Pleasure

City of Power

Agents of The Emperor
Return of The Ancient Ones
Vigilance
Angels of Fire
Kingmaker
The Eight
The Lost Generation
Hunt
Emperor's Council
Speaker of Treachery
Birth Of The Empire
Terraforma
Spaceguard

The Rising Augusta Fantasy Adventure Series
Rise To Power
Rising Walls
Rising Force
Rising Realm

Lord Of War Trilogy (Agents of The Emperor)
Not Scared Of The Dark
Madness
Burn It All Down

Miscellaneous:
RETURN
FREEDOM
SALVATION
Reflection of Mount Flame
The Masked One
The Great Deer
English Independence

OTHER SHORT STORIES BY CONNOR WHITELEY

Mystery Short Story Collections
Criminally Good Stories Volume 1: 20 Detective Mystery Short Stories
Criminally Good Stories Volume 2: 20 Private Investigator Short Stories
Criminally Good Stories Volume 3: 20 Crime Fiction Short Stories
Criminally Good Stories Volume 4: 20 Science Fiction and Fantasy Mystery Short Stories
Criminally Good Stories Volume 5: 20 Romantic Suspense Short Stories

DAMAGE, HEALING, LOVE

Connor Whiteley Starter Collections:
Agents of The Emperor Starter Collection
Bettie English Starter Collection
Matilda Plum Starter Collection
Gay Romance Starter Collection
Way Of The Odyssey Starter Collection
Kendra Detective Fiction Starter Collection

Mystery Short Stories:
Protecting The Woman She Hated
Finding A Royal Friend
Our Woman In Paris
Corrupt Driving
A Prime Assassination
Jubilee Thief
Jubilee, Terror, Celebrations
Negative Jubilation
Ghostly Jubilation
Killing For Womenkind
A Snowy Death
Miracle Of Death
A Spy In Rome
The 12:30 To St Pancreas
A Country In Trouble
A Smokey Way To Go
A Spicy Way To GO
A Marketing Way To Go

A Missing Way To Go
A Showering Way To Go
Poison In The Candy Cane
Kendra Detective Mystery Collection Volume 1
Kendra Detective Mystery Collection Volume 2
Mystery Short Story Collection Volume 1
Mystery Short Story Collection Volume 2
Criminal Performance
Candy Detectives
Key To Birth In The Past

Science Fiction Short Stories:
Their Brave New World
Gummy Bear Detective
The Candy Detective
What Candies Fear
The Blurred Image
Shattered Legions
The First Rememberer
Life of A Rememberer
System of Wonder
Lifesaver
Remarkable Way She Died
The Interrogation of Annabella Stormic
Blade of The Emperor

DAMAGE, HEALING, LOVE

Arbiter's Truth
Computation of Battle
Old One's Wrath
Puppets and Masters
Ship of Plague
Interrogation
Edge of Failure

Fantasy Short Stories:
City of Snow
City of Light
City of Vengeance
Dragons, Goats and Kingdom
Smog The Pathetic Dragon
Don't Go In The Shed
The Tomato Saver
The Remarkable Way She Died
Dragon Coins
Dragon Tea
Dragon Rider

All books in 'An Introductory Series':
Clinical Psychology and Transgender Clients
Clinical Psychology
Careers In Psychology
Psychology of Suicide
Dementia Psychology
Clinical Psychology Reflections Volume 4
Forensic Psychology of Terrorism And
Hostage-Taking
Forensic Psychology of False Allegations
Year In Psychology
CBT For Anxiety
CBT For Depression
Applied Psychology
BIOLOGICAL PSYCHOLOGY 3RD
EDITION
COGNITIVE PSYCHOLOGY THIRD
EDITION
SOCIAL PSYCHOLOGY- 3RD EDITION
ABNORMAL PSYCHOLOGY 3RD
EDITION
PSYCHOLOGY OF RELATIONSHIPS-
3RD EDITION
DEVELOPMENTAL PSYCHOLOGY 3RD
EDITION
HEALTH PSYCHOLOGY
RESEARCH IN PSYCHOLOGY

DAMAGE, HEALING, LOVE

A GUIDE TO MENTAL HEALTH AND
TREATMENT AROUND THE WORLD-
A GLOBAL LOOK AT DEPRESSION
FORENSIC PSYCHOLOGY
THE FORENSIC PSYCHOLOGY OF
THEFT, BURGLARY AND OTHER
CRIMES AGAINST PROPERTY
CRIMINAL PROFILING: A FORENSIC
PSYCHOLOGY GUIDE TO FBI
PROFILING AND GEOGRAPHICAL
AND STATISTICAL PROFILING.
CLINICAL PSYCHOLOGY
FORMULATION IN PSYCHOTHERAPY
PERSONALITY PSYCHOLOGY AND
INDIVIDUAL DIFFERENCES
CLINICAL PSYCHOLOGY
REFLECTIONS VOLUME 2
Clinical Psychology Reflections Volume 3
CULT PSYCHOLOGY
Police Psychology

A Psychology Student's Guide To University
How Does University Work?
A Student's Guide To University And
Learning
University Mental Health and Mindset

Milton Keynes UK
Ingram Content Group UK Ltd.
UKHW021947010924
447661UK00012B/702